Texas Heat

RJ Scott

Love Lane Books

TEXAS HEAT

The Texas series, book 3

© RJ Scott

Copyright 2012-2016 by RJ Scott

Cover design by Meredith Russell

DEDICATION

For Phil and his bacon wrapped aspirin.
And always for my family. I love you.

TRADEMARKS ACKNOWLEDGEMENT

The author acknowledges the trademarked status and trademark owners of the following wordmarks mentioned in this work of fiction:

Armani: Giorgio Armani Group

Ferrari: Ferrari S.p.A., Italy

Hugo Boss: Hugo Boss Fashions Inc, New York

Rolex: Rolex SA

Playboy: Playboy Enterprises International, Inc.

CHAPTER 1

"Riley, can you please try to find Jack?" Donna asked. Unspoken in her words was the plea that Riley keep Jack's temper reined in. No one had to be a rocket scientist to know Jack Campbell-Hayes was *not* taking this whole wedding as well as he was making out. Up until yesterday Jack had been this growly guy who accepted the wedding was happening with as much grace as he could. Then yesterday happened.

What exactly had gone down, no one was sure. Not even Riley could fully understand what was going on in Jack's head. Yesterday he had clammed up and refused to talk at all. Riley knew Jack was happy for his mom; he just couldn't get past the age difference and the money. Donna knew this. Hell, poor Neil Kendrick, Donna's husband-to-be, knew it.

"He was here a minute ago." Riley peered around the kitchen door to the organized chaos beyond the window in the front of the Double D. Looking for the familiar figure of his husband proved fruitless. There was no sign of Jack.

"Where's Neil?" Riley asked.

Donna shook her head and Riley wished he had never asked. Whatever was happening between Jack and Neil was something Donna didn't need spilling over onto her wedding day. Donna laid a gentle hand on Riley's arm and instinctively he pulled her closer for a hug. She smelled of sunshine and home, and peace flooded him at the scent. Dressed in a robe, she wasn't in her wedding finery or whatever she was wearing today, but her hair was twisted up into a knot at the top of her head. When he stepped back he didn't think he had seen anyone more beautiful than the woman who had gifted the world with Jack Campbell.

His job on this cool Valentine's Day was to keep the peace. Although Jack and Neil had made some kind of unspoken promise to not fight it didn't mean that Riley's hot-tempered husband wasn't off somewhere releasing tension on some poor unsuspecting caterer.

"I'll find him," he promised.

"Everything okay here?"

Both he and Donna turned to face a concerned Beth. Emily, her daughter, was gripping her hand tightly. Walking now and with as much sass as her Uncle Jack, Emily was a breath of fresh air in the room. Donna immediately scooped her granddaughter up in her arms and squeezed her until she giggled uncontrollably.

"Gramma, you coming?"

Riley turned at Hayley's words. His daughter's voice was so familiar and gentle and he couldn't stop the surge of love for the nine-year-old that had put herself in charge of getting Gramma ready for her wedding.

"Hey, pumpkin," Riley said.

"Daddy, you shouldn't be in here," she said.

Riley raised his hands in defense. "I'm going, I'm going."

Somehow Hayley had Beth, and Emily had Donna moving away and out of the kitchen into the good room. The front room was where Donna's bridal party were readying themselves.

Sighing, Riley left the kitchen and moved outside, down the steps to the front of the house. He cast a thorough glance around the area but couldn't see the strong figure of his husband anywhere. He could, however, see Neil who was standing to one side with a group of guys. The man looked to be unhurt and upright so Riley surmised Jack hadn't been in that direction. Exchanging waves with Josh, who was across the yard, pacing and looking down at cards in his hand, Riley weaved through caterers and visitors until he reached his brother-in-law's side.

"Have you seen Jack?" he asked.

Josh's eyes widened at the question and he looked behind him to where Neil was standing. He visibly relaxed that the bridegroom was still there and wasn't face-planted in the dirt at Jack's hand. Jack and Neil's uneasy truce had been tested more and more the closer the wedding came.

"He said something a while ago about the caterers and their vans blocking the horses."

"Are they?"

"Are they what?" Josh was distracted. Being the man who was giving his mom away was not coming easily to him and he was way past nervous.

"Blocking in the horses?"

"No." Josh frowned. "They're over on the other side by the new barn."

Riley turned on his heel and headed to the only other place that he thought his husband could be. Crossing to the old barn, their barn, he was relieved to see the still figure of Jack leaning on an old stable wall with his head tilted back and his eyes closed.

"Jack?" Riley cleared the short distance between them until he was toe-to-toe with Jack. His husband was dressed and ready for the wedding and he looked so damn gorgeous. He was lucky Riley was on a mission or he would be out of those clothes in an instant.

A soft gray suit fit Jack snuggly and the jacket hung perfectly on Jack's broad shoulders. A Western-style belt buckle was the only concession to cowboy that Riley could see, and tucking a finger behind the belt, he leaned into the man who owned him from his heart outward. Jack had shaved but it was a matter of a few hours before stubble defined his jaw and heat caused his unruly dark hair to fall in disarray around his head. Riley loved that hair and the stubble; the burn of it against his skin when they made love was exquisite. Questioning blue eyes, the color of a cloudless Texas sky, looked up at him and Riley smiled in reassurance.

"Why are you hiding?" Riley asked.

Jack pulled Riley the final inch until he was supporting his husband's weight. He was wearing aftershave and Riley could see a tiny nick in his tanned skin on his defined cheekbone. Carefully he placed a gentle kiss on the mark.

"'M not hiding," Jack drawled.

"You *are* hiding," Riley said. He knew his other half too well.

Jack shrugged but said nothing. That was not a good sign. Jack clamming up and not talking was a recipe for disaster.

"Jack? Talk to me?" Riley used his free hand to cup Jack's cheek and pressed firmly when Jack turned his head slightly into the touch. There was something in his cornflower eyes—uncertainty maybe?

"Neil came to see me yesterday with a prenup he wanted me to take a look at."

Riley wasn't surprised. Jack was not only worried about the age gap between his mom and the younger veterinarian but also about any and all money and property in his mom's name that the guy would have access to as her new husband. Riley, on the other hand, thought Neil was a good guy; he loved Donna to distraction, despite the twenty-year difference.

Riley cursed that, with Jack increasing the horse training side of the D and with him so involved in the latest Hayes Oil project, they had lost track of each other over the last few days. Damn it. If he had been here when Neil visited to speak to Jack then maybe he could have smoothed things over.

"A prenup is a good thing. Right?" Riley leaned in a little more and it felt right when Jack circled his waist with his arms, both of his large capable hands resting on his lower back. He could feel the flex of his lover's muscles in his broad chest and it didn't matter that a hundred people were only thirty feet away around the side of the barn; he really wanted Jack.

"No," Jack responded simply. "He talked to me and he was defensive and I tried to tell him that I trusted my mom and her choices but he didn't listen. Just kept asking me to read the prenup and telling me I should get my lawyers to look at it to make sure."

"He's gonna be defensive, Jack. He knows how you feel about him."

"Well, what if I didn't?"

"Didn't?" Riley wasn't following this change in direction.

"What if I felt that he was good for Mom and that I even liked the guy a bit."

Riley watched as Jack worried at his lower lip with his teeth. This wasn't Jack. Jack knew his place in the world and was certain of his feelings. He didn't wander from one point of view to another; he was black and white.

"What did the prenup say?" Riley decided this was a better thing to focus on.

"That he'd have me, Beth, or Josh sign off on anything financial with Mom, that at any time any one of us could call in an independent audit on her money." Jack stopped talking and leaned his head forward to rest his forehead on Riley's chest.

"That's a bad thing?"

"Yes." Jack's voice was muffled. "All I want for my mom is a strong man who will look after her and make her happy. If he signs that prenup then all that is left is half a man with no control over his life and sons-in-law who don't trust him. It just looks like we don't trust Mom to know her own mind and hell"—he lifted his head and his eyes were full of fire—"do you know of any woman anywhere who is stronger than Donna Campbell?"

Riley shook his head. "So what happened then?"

"He gave this speech about how he just wanted Mom to be happy and left me the papers. He's signed them; all I need to do is sign them, get Beth and Josh to do so, and then we can get the whole lot notarized. He assumed that is what I was doing and then he shook my hand and said he was proud to be a part of our family."

"Did you get it notarized?"

"No. I didn't show Josh or Beth and I didn't even sign the fucking thing. How can I do that and then look Mom in the face?"

"So, wait, you haven't signed, you think Neil is good for your mom, and you trust him."

With a groan Jack rested his forehead back on Riley's chest again. There was a muttered "fuck" and Riley thought on what he had to say here. Damn his obstinate husband.

"Okay, cowboy. Where is the paperwork?"

"Inthetruck." Jack ran his words together.

"Get the paperwork then decide. Sign and it's done or don't sign and tell Neil what you really think." Riley checked his watch. "There's thirty minutes until the ceremony starts, plenty of time to get your head out of your ass and do something to make this right."

Jack groaned again and Riley smiled. His cowboy may be a stubborn fucker but Jack knew what he had to do. He lifted his face again, but this time worry had been replaced by something else—something punctuated by the press of a hard and very interested dick against Riley's thigh. Jack quirked his eyebrows.

"Have we got time for—"

"No," Riley replied adamantly. As much as he wanted Jack out of the suit and bent over the nearest rail, they had things to do that were more important.

"Not even a—"

"No."

"You're a fucking bastard, Riley Campbell-Hayes," Jack said with no heat.

"It's why you love me." Riley smirked. "You have half an hour."

* * * * *

Jack hated it when Riley was right. Inevitably Riley was always freaking right when Jack came out of his stubborn focused stage. *The fucker.*

He readjusted himself and saw the lick of heat in Riley's eyes. If only they had longer then falling to his knees and wringing a noisy, messy orgasm from his suit-wearing husband would have been right at the top of his list.

He chuckled and pulled Riley close for a kiss, a touch filled with the promise of later. Finally separating, Jack left to get the papers from the truck and with them safely in his hand he returned to the throng to find his soon-to-be whatever. Certainly not step-daddy, but something a little more official than the guy who was keeping his momma's bed warm at night.

He saw Neil's eyes widen when he approached and guilt twisted in his gut. The man had a couple of other guys with him, two in suits and one dressed in Sunday-best Cowboy. Nice-looking guy, built like a brick outhouse, with short blond hair and dark blue eyes. This guy took a careful step forward to put himself closer to Jack. He wasn't actually between Jack and Neil but it was enough of a stance to be meaningful. They stood toe-to-toe for a few seconds and it was humiliating to think that this cowboy was feeling the need to protect Neil from him.

"Is everything okay?" Neil finally asked.

"Can we talk?" Jack asked formally. The other two men in suits moved away, leaving Neil and the cowboy in front of him.

Neil shook his head. "Please don't. Not now. Can it wait until after?" he asked simply.

The cowboy frowned at Neil's words. Hell, who wouldn't. Neil sounded resigned and just a little pissed. If this cowboy was a good friend then he probably knew everything. Jack wasn't going to let this lie.

"I wanted to apologize for my behavior," Jack said firmly. He knew it was his imagination but he felt as if every eye of the waiting wedding party was on him. *What the hell?* He had told Neil what he thought of him in public before, it was only right to be telling the man now how Jack had changed his mind. "And I have a wedding gift for you."

He thrust the paperwork of the prenup at Neil, and the man looked down at it with resignation on his face.

"Thank you," he said carefully. He didn't immediately take the papers. Jack shook them a little to encourage Neil to take them and at first he didn't get why the guy wasn't snatching them out of his hands. Then realization hit him. Neil probably thought it was the signed and notarized paperwork. *Fuck. When am I going to do things right?*

"I didn't—" he started. Then he thought maybe actions spoke louder than words. Taking the thick sheaf of papers, he ripped them cleanly down the middle and then ripped each half again. Finally, grasping the pieces in one hand, he held them back out to Neil who accepted them in his left hand. The man was obviously shocked, judging from his facial expression. Although he was quiet, his expressive eyes spoke volumes.

"Thank you, Jack," Neil said. His voice was gentle and then he held out his right hand. Jack hesitated briefly in accepting the handshake. Didn't seem right welcoming the man into his family with a freaking handshake. With a single step forward he pulled the other man into a close hug that Neil returned immediately.

"Welcome to the family, Neil," Jack said. He stepped back and inclined his head to the cowboy at Neil's side and then with what he was sure was every eye on him, he left to find somewhere to hide again until the wedding began.

* * * * *

The ceremony was beautiful. Donna looked radiant in a lacy summer dress in a pale shade of blue and Neil was smiling so hard that Jack thought the guy could do permanent damage to his face.

Hayley and little Emily were flower girls and Josh's daughter Lea made it three. Lea's older brother Logan was thirteen now and wasn't that keen on being labeled as anything except 'cool dude in a suit' but he did hold Emily's hand the entire service.

Jack couldn't take his eyes off of Hayley. She was taller now, coming up on ten in September; she was the spitting image of her dad with the same blond hair and hazel eyes.

He couldn't be prouder of Riley's daughter. She was his as well and she loved her Pappa as much as she loved Riley.

The backdrop to this wedding was home. The beautiful ranch in the setting sun with the vista of their land spreading before him was where his heart felt most at peace. Feet planted firmly on Texan soil with his family around him, Jack was at rest.

Riley slipped a hand into his. "This reminds me of when we renewed our vows," he murmured.

"I love you, het-boy," Jack replied softly so no one could hear.

"I love you too, cowboy."

Jack was only one step away from letting an emotional sigh leave him. This land, these people, they were his and he was theirs. That was the way he was and the way he always would be.

CHAPTER 2

Robbie Curtis wandered away from the main gathering. Neil Kendrick, his best friend since grade school was now married to a woman whom he loved more than life itself and to Robbie that was a fine thing to have. Neil had made a good choice in Donna and forever-loyal-to-his-friend Robbie could have told the 'big and hulking guy' that Donna had made a good choice in the ever-loyal Neil. Apparently 'big and hulking' had a name. Jack Campbell-Hayes. Married to some guy called Riley. Married. Two dudes.

Hard enough to take a step out of the closet in his line of work, let alone enter into a gay marriage. The guys who had beaten up his ex, well, they'd be on him quicker than flies on shit.

He'd wandered past the general groups of well-wishers, inclining his head whenever he was spoken to, and eventually managed to escape the celebrations and make his way to the barns at the rear of the house. No one stopped him and anyway, he was much happier with horses than he was around people. He was curious; apparently this spread dealt with breeding and Neil spoke about how there was expansion into training good solid quarter horses.

Leaning against the closest stall he was face-to-face with a beautiful bay. He crooned low and extended a hand to her in greeting and she snuffled his open hand before shaking her head and taking a step back. Robbie laughed, she was definitely flirting with him as she nudged up against him.

"Hello, beautiful," he whispered. Her ears flattened and then perked up. "Why aren't you out on all this gorgeous space?" Unconcerned by what he was saying and instead intent on nuzzling him, he laughed at the horse's unashamed request for fuss. He'd only left Australia a week before, had only said goodbye to all he knew and loved there a simple seven days earlier. But the scent here, the horses and the hay, made him long for the place he used to call home. Neil was going to hook him up with some part-time work. Hell, his friend had said that at the end of the day he could learn to assist Neil. Robbie didn't do well with charity, even that offered by his oldest friend—the man he called his brother. He guessed though he didn't really have a lot of options and was glad to have at least one friend back here in the States.

He glanced up the row of stables and counted a minimum of six spaces. The stables were clean and well cared for. In fact, the fencing, the stables, and everything to do with the ranch operation was a lot cleaner and sturdier than the ranch house itself, which was looking a little tired—not to mention the potholed road leading to the house. So many things here reminded Robbie of home. When a ranch put everything they had into the welfare of the horses and the livestock then you knew it was a good place to stand.

"Solo-Alexandra." The voice from behind startled him. Robbie cursed himself for his inattention. It was things like this that got a man in trouble. He slowly turned to face the man whose voice he recognized. Hmmm. Big and hulking, aka Jack Campbell-Hayes, one of the married guys.

"Sorry?"

"Alex for short. Her momma is this beauty, Solo-Cal." Jack was indicating a gorgeous sorrel mare pushing at his arm for attention.

"Beautiful horses." Robbie wasn't sure what else to say. Neil had tried his hardest with Jack, but Robbie had seen one too many drunken emails from his friend demanding to know why Jack hated him. Well, for Robbie, someone hurting his friend riled him.

"Almost lost them both a while back in a fire," Jack continued.

"Neil told me." No point in letting Jack think that Neil hadn't told him every damn thing concerning the Double D.

"I'm not placing your accent." Jack was frowning. He was a good-looking guy, and a frown darkening his blue eyes wasn't a good look. He was everything Robbie avoided. First he was a cowboy, a stubborn one at that, and second he was a strong guy and could probably drop Robbie to the ground in a heartbeat. After everything that had gone down back home Robbie had learned his lesson. No cowboys. No big cowboys.

"Wyoming born and bred, Australia for the past ten years," he finally answered reluctantly. Social skills escaped him.

"Australia?"

"As a buckaroo, a cowboy, working with quarter horses on a spread in the Northern Territories, some three thousand acres."

"The D is eight hundred acres," Jack mused. "Australia, eh? That explains the accent, I guess." Jack lifted a booted foot and rested it on a wooden crossbar below Alex's stall door. "Definitely a tinge of something other than American in there."

For a few minutes the two men looked in on the horses in a near companionable silence. Robbie wasn't entirely sure what to say. He had a lot of questions inside him. Neil had said Jack was expanding the training side of the ranch. Did that mean he was training horses for rodeo and show or for working on ranches? Robbie had a list of questions in his head and he was concentrating on how to word them when they were interrupted.

"Hey, gorgeous." Jack turned with a grin and Robbie watched as way-tall-dude, the other half of the Campbell-Hayes couple, near pounced on Jack. Clearly Robbie hadn't been spotted if the way Riley was grinding up against Jack was any indication. "Knew you'd be hidin' out here."

Was it Robbie's imagination or was Riley's voice a little slurred?

"How much champagne did you swallow?" Jack asked with a grin.

"Enough to fuck you here and now in front of everyone," Riley answered. His tone was deadly serious.

"We have company," Jack explained. Riley didn't stop with the hugging and pulling but he did at least look over his shoulder at Robbie. His eyes widened and then he extricated himself from Jack with a rearrangement of his groin area. Robbie pretended not to notice. Riley was gorgeous up close. He'd seen photos, he had Internet, and he had followed the whole soap opera that was their lives from murder to barns being burned to marriages to hostage situations. Where Jack was all holy-hot-as-hell cowboy, Riley was wearing that suit like he'd been born into it. He was leaning into Jack and Jack wasn't moving away or keeping any distance between them. If anything, Jack had an arm around his husband and was pulling him closer. Riley certainly seemed to sober quickly and Robbie wondered how much was alcohol and how much was playing.

"Don't mind me," Robbie said quickly. Silence. *Fuck.* What the hell had he just said? He was trying to be clever and funny and instead had come over as some kind of voyeuristic pervert. He waited for either man to say something, anything. In fact, he tensed in expectation of being beaten to the ground. Every muscle tightened in anticipation of the need to defend himself.

Jack simply looked up at Riley, who was smiling broadly.

"Nah," he said. "Let me take this big lug indoors. Nice to meet you, Robbie." Jack extended his right hand and Robbie rubbed his own on his best jeans before shaking Jack's hand. When Riley did the same Robbie shook and then took a step backward. He left the barn, walked around the corner, and leaned back against the wall. He wasn't far enough away not to be able to hear Jack and Riley talking but he couldn't make out whole words. Sighing, he turned to go find Neil and make his excuses. When he passed the open barn door he couldn't have stopped himself from looking in if he'd tried.

Riley and Jack were locked so closely in an embrace you couldn't see light between them. Riley had his head tilted back and Jack was tracing a path of kisses from jaw to throat. When Riley let out a groan of need and pushed Jack away from him and back against the barn wall it was possibly the most erotic thing Robbie had ever seen. Flushed and harder than he had been in days he left the area as quickly as he could. Shame at his reaction conflicted with the lust inside him.

He had never missed Paul more than he did today.

* * * * *

Riley's gift to Donna and Neil was a week on the same island that he and Jack had been on when they first heard that Riley was a dad. When he initially broached the subject with Jack he had expected some kind of resistance, but Jack smiled and said that the whole idea was a good one. Not one word about the amount of money Riley was using on the gift.

The guests were grouped around the limo that Josh had been responsible for organizing. It had been decorated with ribbons and balloons. Riley didn't envy Donna and Neil the trip to the airstrip, where the Hayes jet sat ready and waiting, with that much crap advertising their just-wed status.

Everyone was waving as the car pulled away and no one moved until the vehicle was nothing but a trail of dust in the air to mark its passing.

"That was a lovely wedding." Eden sighed. Riley pulled her closer for a hug. Her boyfriend, Sean, was a long-term partner but he had yet to pop any kind of question of marriage. As a journalist he was very seldom in Texas and their time apart was more and more frequent. He hadn't made it to the wedding today or indeed stepped foot anywhere near Eden for a month. Riley liked the guy. Well, he liked him as much as any big brother liked a sister's lover. But he couldn't be the only one who was wondering why he was away so much and why it was taking this long to settle down and propose to Eden. Maybe he had gotten cold feet? Maybe he had someone else? Riley didn't vocalize his fears.

She turned in his arms and hugged him close.

"Hey, are you okay?" Riley asked.

"I'm fine. Can't a sister grab some brother time now and then?"

Riley laughed and hugged her even tighter. He was a good foot taller than her and she was soon in a position of finding it hard to breathe. He released her when she punched him in the thigh with her free hand and in a flash brother/sister was normal and on an even keel.

"Are you staying?" Riley asked.

"I'm going with Mom and Jim but I'll be back tomorrow to help clean up."

Riley glanced at his watch. The midnight hour was close and he stifled a yawn.

"We have a crew doing that, but I know Hayley would love for you to come over."

Jack stepped into their small circle and prized Eden away from Riley.

"My turn, brother-in-law privilege," he insisted.

Laughing, she cuddled in close.

"Are you staying?" Jack repeated Riley's question.

"She's going back with Mom and Dad," Riley answered for her.

Jack raised his eyebrows over Eden's head. Riley knew exactly what his husband was thinking. With the Hayes side of the family gone and with the Campbells just down to Hayley and the two of them, it meant that for the first time in many weeks they had the ranch nearly to themselves.

"Do you think Hayley would like a sleepover with her aunty?" Eden asked. Her voice was muffled against Jack's chest and she pushed away. "I don't want today to end and we could go shopping tomorrow." She brightened at the thought.

Riley tried to be the responsible parent. The last he had seen of Hayley she had been running circles around her cousin Logan, who watched her with that tolerant patience only a family member could find. For some reason she had latched on to Josh's eldest boy and it was a hundred kinds of cute to see Jack's nephew so happy to be with Hayley.

"I'll go find and ask her." Eden said this without waiting for an answer and quickly walked away to find her niece.

In small groups the guests left, then Eden with a hyper Hayley, followed by the caterers, and finally the group of cleaners that had left the ranch looking nearly as normal as it could be after hosting an event like a wedding.

Paparazzi had stayed away from the event, at least off of Double D property, and no helicopters had been seen, although Riley did wonder what kind of journalistic crowd people leaving had to get through to get off of the D. When finally it was just the two of them Riley felt relieved and expectant. A whole night with the buzz of champagne in his blood and his sexy husband within reach was surely a recipe for only one thing.

In unison they turned to each other.

"I'll check the horses—"

"I'll be in the barn—"

Jack gripped Riley's jacket and reeled him in for a hard kiss.

"Gimme ten," Jack groaned.

"Make it five, cowboy."

CHAPTER 3

Riley stretched in bed. Last night had been the first night they'd been alone in the house since Donna's wedding in February, and now they were so far into July that February seemed a long time ago. God bless Eden and her shopping trips enabling them to get some time alone. Last night had been so intense and he realized just how much time he was spending at work and away from home. That had to stop.

The early morning sun was bright through the partially drawn drapes and the combination of that and the sound of an alarm was pulling Jack from sleep.

"Your cell," Jack murmured against his arm. Riley leaned over and stole a kiss from his sleepy husband. The screen flashed with a voicemail and he pressed the button to play it on speaker.

"Hi. This is a message for Riley. Uhmmm. I don't know if he'll remember me but I shared a house with him off campus for a while? My name is Elijah Martin. I majored in business, minored in fucking up? I read this article about him... wait... you don't need to know that. Just. Can you maybe give him this message and give me a call back at some point? Thanks. Bye."

"Whozat?" Jack mumbled. Evidently his question was rhetorical as he moved in his sleep and settled again with a low snore. Riley eased himself back on his side of the bed, still as close to Jack as he could get, and clutched his cell to his chest. Elijah Martin, or Eli as Riley had known him. Wow. That was a blast from the past.

Riley remembered he was sassy and fun and short. Although considering his own height that wasn't difficult. Dark-haired and green-eyed with a small and lithe body, pre-Jack Riley may well have wanted to get to know him better if he hadn't been moving from one conquest to another throughout college. Well, pre-Jack Riley had not been done chasing girls so no, he wouldn't have gone near sexy, alluring Eli with a stick.

Eli was the product of a fucked-up family similar to Riley's. Riley recalled a dad who was in prison for some drug dealing shit and a mom who had featured in some kind of guys mag spread at the age of forty entirely nude except for a boa constrictor draped over her ample chest. Yep. Just as fucked-up as the Hayes family. He placed the cell on his bedside cabinet, crossed his arms behind his head, and closed his eyes. Sleeping with his husband was usually so easy but college memories flooded back in a rush.

Unsettled, he slowly rolled out of bed, and pulling on shorts, he moved as quietly as he could out of the room, taking his cell. Checking in on Hayley's room was instinctive and he chuckled to himself when he didn't see the familiar lump under the piled quilt. Having time alone with Jack was pretty freaking good but breakfast with Hayley was something special. He would never admit it but even with the hot sweaty sex and alone time he missed her. He couldn't really remember a time when she wasn't part of his life, of their life.

Recently he had been thinking maybe she needed a little sister or brother. What Riley wouldn't give for a miniature Jack running around the house all piss and vinegar and giving them a run for their money. *Something to talk about with Jack later maybe?* His husband had never mentioned a bigger family but then to be fair neither had Riley. Maybe it was time to at least say yes or no to the idea. Riley was about to turn thirty soon, not that he was counting the days or anything, but he didn't want to be too old to be a dad.

After making coffee he took that and the cell out to the new morning. The clock in the kitchen said six-thirty and briefly Riley considered leaving calling until later. The consideration took little more than a few seconds before he was pressing redial on Eli's number. Fucker needed repaying for the number of pranks he'd played on Riley in college.

"'Lo." The voice answered on the third ring.

Riley wasn't entirely sure this was Eli but whoever it was didn't sound sleepy.

"Eli? It's Riley. Riley Campbell-Hayes."

"Riley! Hey. Hang on a minute." Eli was clearly moving out of wherever he was and into an open area as the quality of the call changed from echoing to clear. "Still there?" he inquired.

"Still here."

"Sorry. Staying with Mom and she's entertaining." Eli imbued the word 'entertaining' with what Riley imagined was a raise of his eyebrows and a shake of his head. Eli had long ago given up on his exhibitionist mom who put the F in MILF.

"Sorry to call you back so early in the day," Riley started.

"No problems. I'm still on UK time. Only flew back in to the US a few days ago and my clock is all over the place. Sleep is not my friend. How are you?"

"Doing good."

"I read all the stuff that happened in the last few years."

"Yeah?"

"Sorry about your loss."

Riley wasn't sure which loss Eli was referring to. His brother? His dad? Hayes Oil? Instead he gave a standard, and very safe, answer.

"Thank you."

"And sorry I didn't... you know... contact you to give support and shit but I had some stuff of my own going on."

Typical Eli. Flighty, incorrigible, but at least freaking honest. Riley decided he wasn't ready to face that particular elephant in the room and instead changed the subject.

"How are you?" Riley asked. He wasn't sure what else to say so he guessed it was best to stick with the usual pleasantries until he could see if the old friendship was still alive.

"Usual shit. Got asked to leave London for a slight indecent exposure misunderstanding," Eli said.

Riley snorted a laugh. At that point, despite the eight-year gap since they had talked, they dropped the formalities and were once again back as pledges and causing shit together. The last time they had spoken, or rather argued, was the discussion that had driven the wedge. Neither mentioned it. Riley wasn't sure he ever wanted it brought up again. Especially considering the focus of it.

"They threw you out?"

"More encouraged me to leave. Said, and I quote, 'the UK will not accept behavior on Palace grounds such as what they had witnessed'."

"*Palace* grounds?"

"In my defense I didn't know. I mean, where was the security if I managed to get over the wall? I was coming home anyway. London I love, but Texas is home."

They talked about college, and Hayley, and Jack. Riley ended up inviting Eli over for dinner that night and as easy as that the old friends had healed a rift far too childish to even consider as anything important now. Riley couldn't even remember exactly what it was that had been said the day Eli left college. Something about a boyfriend who was giving Eli grief and it was somehow connected to Lexie and Riley. Maybe they could cover that when they talked.

"I have a favor to ask of you though. But that isn't why I reconnected. I was going to get in touch with you as soon as I got settled." Eli was rambling. "Only something happened that upped the timescale a bit. I just think this could be good for you and your husband and for the ranch and—"

"Spit it out. Jeez, you haven't changed a bit, have you?" Riley smiled. This was the Eli he remembered, all big explanations and plans and in-your-face demands. The whole package wrapped up in Eli's lithe figure had always been so much fun.

"I kind of found my niche in London. You remember my camera?"

Remember it? Riley hated the damn thing. God help him if any of the photos Eli took at college were leaked to the press. He recalled Eli had been good at photography though.

"I do," he answered.

"Well, it's a career now." The normally boisterous guy sounded simply proud of himself. That was a change. Half of Eli's issues at college were because he felt he had something to prove to anyone and everyone. That he was faster, better, or bolder. And every time he ended up just being the one in the most trouble; hence his early exit from the college. "I've been asked to create a marketing suite of photos for an underwear company."

"Okay?" Riley posed a whole raft of questions in that simple word.

"How would your husband feel about using the Double D as a backdrop? Nothing identifiable to him or you," he hastened to add. "But barns, horses, y'know, cowboy stuff."

"Cowboy stuff," Riley said. He couldn't help the snort of laughter. Luckily Eli didn't take offense and was laughing alongside him.

"Why us then?"

Eli sighed. "There is still so much shit flying around about gay cowboys and getting spreads to agree to have me and twenty near-naked men on their property plus all the extra stuff is nigh on impossible."

"But you think because of the fact Jack is my husband that I will be able to influence a decision?" Riley considered the evidence in the proposal. Jack wasn't hidden in any sense of the word but he was very much a man's man and liked his privacy.

"Also I would get to catch up with you. Couple weeks is all, in mid-September."

"I'll ask him. We'll have an answer for you at dinner."

* * * * *

Dinner was boisterous and noisy and that was just Eli and Hayley. They hit it off immediately, especially when Eli admitted he knew Hayley's mom.

"So your dad was standing up and giving this huge speech about boom and bust, it was part of an end of course assessment, and he was using all these cool words." Eli used air quotes around the word cool and Hayley laughed. This was despite the fact she probably didn't understand half of what Eli was talking about. Riley simply groaned and sank lower in his seat. He cast a quick look at Jack who was sipping coffee and alternating between loud guffaws of laughter and wicked grins he was sending Riley's way. "Then he uses this one explanation and it's something like... hell, I can't recall."

"Equilibrium price," Riley supplied. He remembered the day as if it was yesterday. On the chart of embarrassing moments it was pretty much up there.

"Oh my—yes." Eli threw back his head with a loud laugh. "So your mom is in the front row and your dad here has been liking her from afar for months and she won't give him the time of day. So I don't know what happened but he couldn't get the word equilibrium right. And your mom corrected him. She told him loudly and firmly how to pronounce it."

"She was clever," Hayley said.

Riley looked across at his daughter who was leaning against Jack. She didn't appear sad to be talking about her mom. Maybe he should tell her more things that only he could know.

"So clever," Eli agreed. "So, your dad here, he was steaming. Bright red as well—"

"Like when he gets all angry about football and shouts at the TV?" Hayley was all innocence but Riley could see the spark of mischief in his daughter's beautiful eyes.

"Don't get me started on football," Eli said with a laugh. "You would not believe the stories I have about your dad from college."

"Did my mom fall in love with my dad over saying that word?" Hayley asked.

To give him his due Eli didn't falter in his answer which was immediate and firm.

"Your mom fell in love with your dad the first day she saw him. Your dad did the same, he just didn't know it."

* * * * *

Riley leaned into Jack and wrapped an arm around his husband's waist as they waved Eli off.

"What did I agree to?" Jack asked. He looked a little stunned but Riley wouldn't have expected anything else. Eli was very definitely a force to be reckoned with.

"Twenty half-naked male models draped over your fences and scaring the horses." Riley shook his head as he said this. "You've been Eli-ed."

"He seems like a nice guy though. Hayley liked him. I liked him." Jack sounded thoughtful. Riley was still in shock that his husband had agreed to the shoot in the small space between steaks and dessert.

"It didn't worry you him telling stories about Lexie?" *I don't want him to tell you anything that will make you doubt what we have.*

The taillights of Eli's rental finally disappeared and Jack simply wriggled free of Riley's hold and turned to face him. His expression was serious and Riley suddenly felt a little uncomfortable, but nothing could make Riley break the gaze.

"Lexie is Hayley's mom," Jack began. His tone was soft but firm. "I want Hayley to know as much as she can about her, and I want to know more about you. I'm not insecure, het-boy. I know you love me and I love you. The history of you is always a good place to learn how you got to be so damn perfect for me."

Riley sighed and buried his face against Jack's shoulder.

"How come you always know what to say?"

"Practice." Jack laughed. "I had a thought that maybe Eli could stay when he's here for the shoot."

"In the house?"

"May as well. We can stand to have a friend of yours stay a while."

"No naked monkey-sex in the barn? For two whole weeks? Can you manage that?" Riley was joking but Jack's answer was deadly serious.

"You don't have many friends here to visit, Riley. It would be good for us all to get to know Eli. Anyway"— Jack smirked—"we can just be very quiet and make love when he's asleep."

"Not before we check for cameras," Riley deadpanned.

"He didn't?"

"My room. Time-lapse images of quite a few things you don't want the rest of the world knowing about."

"I'm assuming he deleted them?"

"Yeah. I made him."

Jack leaned close. His breath held the lulling, gentle scent of fine whiskey. Riley was pulled to him like a magnet with a desperate and sudden need to touch.

"Shame. Could have been good to watch."

In seconds Riley was hard and ready. Christ, what this man did to him. It should be illegal.

CHAPTER 4

Today had been one of the longest days on record. Meetings ran into conference calls and Riley hadn't managed to grab much more than a cookie with his endless cups of coffee. The group of five men still hadn't managed to get to a final agreement on the bids. Twelve tracts of undersea exploration rights were up for grabs and Riley had a gut feeling about two of them. His new company promoted ethical exploration and alternative energies; every member of staff from accountant to diver shared in successes and failures, and that invariably meant Riley dealing with much more than just his first love.

His map room at his new office sat silent and he wanted nothing more than to be in the cool room, cross-legged on the floor, studying maps and charting core samples. He really did not want to be sitting in this room with a bunch of old men who wouldn't know ethical exploration if it was lubed and stuck up their asses.

Not one of them had what Riley had. That frisson of excitement when he followed a seam in the seabed and his instincts, checked deposits, and then found oil reserves was a natural high. Something his dad and his brother had never really understood and evidently something these idiots failed to grasp. Riley couldn't understand it. He loved the research and the knowledge you needed to do well. The office and the negotiation and the endless back and forth of the discussion between the men sitting here with him was driving him insane. He looked over at Jim thoughtfully. Having his dad here provided more support than Riley could have ever thought. Jim was so involved in CH and really, they were making up for lost time. For so long he'd thought Gerald Hayes was his father—he was never happier than when he found out that Jim was his real dad. Jim sat calmly and quietly to one side and was making notes on paper in front of him. Ostensibly he was there on Riley's behalf, as counsel and secretary to this deal.

They'd had all the big meetings for this proposal and Riley thought everything had been agreed to. Then all of a sudden out of thin air Josiah 'pompous ass' Harrold from the large and, some would say, unwieldy Santone Corp called this urgent meeting to discuss, of all things, percentage returns.

"All I am saying," Josiah started, "is that, in view of the fact that CH is a new face in oil, a lower percentage of any returns is what you should expect."

"There's forty-three years' experience in this company," Riley summarized. He forced himself to remain calm. Like the other three men in the room, Josiah was a contemporary of Gerald and Jack's dad. Josiah knew exactly how long Hayes Oil had been in existence and how much of the Hayes name and experience had gone into Riley's new venture.

"Yes, but no offense is meant by this at all. If it had been your dad or Jeff sitting here..." Josiah's voice deliberately trailed away and he looked at Riley pointedly. Riley was damn sure Josiah meant every single little inflection in his voice as a means to offend. Anger coiled in his spine and he dug his fingers into his thighs, letting the pain ground him and help him to remember to bite his tongue. He counted backwards from ten, a trick he had learned from many occasions in an office similar to this with his dad or brother.

Think before you speak, Riley. Keep the moral high ground. Don't back down.

"I'm not entering negotiations here, Josiah." Riley deliberately used the other man's name. Josiah's lip curled. He had always been Mr Harrold up until a few years back and Riley got the impression the man wasn't that fond of this new level playing field that put CH on the same starting page as Santone Corp with the current negotiations. "CH will be underwriting the same risk as the other four in this syndicate. Does anyone else have an issue regarding perceived investment and reward?"

Riley turned directly to the other men. He knew them all in one way or another.

"No issues here."

"We're ready to sign."

The assurances were quick and to the point and Josiah really had nowhere to go. Without him the finances would be tight but Riley had some reserves and hell, if it meant getting this bid in on time, he would forego any percentage over and above covering his own costs. He wasn't going to let Josiah know this though.

"Josiah?" he prompted helpfully. The man was bright red in the face and Riley did, for one minute, think that pride would overcome his innate greediness.

"I never said I had an issue—"

"Good," Riley interrupted. "I'll have the papers couriered to your offices by midday tomorrow with a view to having everything in place by Friday. Is that doable?"

Three yeses, and a reluctant scowl from Josiah, were his answer. Riley exchanged a quick nod with his dad—he knew they would talk later in private about the worries both had where Santone Corp was concerned. Santone was like Hayes Oil under Gerald Hayes, unwieldy, corrupt, and a hundred other problems. If Riley had a choice he wouldn't be dealing with Josiah or Santone, but it had been Santone who had approached him and he knew the weight of the company's name on his proposal would look good. Riley hoped that doing things his way would show Josiah how *good* oil business could be done. Jim doubted it, but at least the Santone investment was in name only with Riley and his team providing the actual ground work for the whole thing. They stood and Riley exchanged pleasantries until finally his dad and the others left leaving only Riley and a hovering Josiah remaining at the open door. Riley tensed when Josiah leaned forward, his florid face purpled across his cheekbones and his fists balled at his sides.

"You daddy always warned me you were ineffective and weak. If your research isn't sound and you are screwing us all over, then I swear I will take you down just like Gerald wanted to."

"Gerald is dead, Josiah." Riley was not rising to this.

"Don't fuck this up, Hayes." Josiah leaned back with the glitter of triumph in his eyes. He was leaving having had the last word and saying what he wanted to say.

"Campbell-Hayes," Riley said softly but firmly. "My name is Campbell-Hayes."

If anything Josiah's contemptuous expression rose a notch. He said nothing though. Standing toe-to-toe, Riley had a foot in height on him and God knows how much toned muscle where Josiah had turned to fat. With a huff Josiah walked out of the reception area toward the exit and Riley watched from behind his pet Yucca plant. When the doors opened Josiah pushed out and Riley was never happier to see who walked in seconds afterwards.

Jack.

Jack with his hat in his hand and the dirt and dust of work on his skin and the widest of grins on his face. They said nothing as Riley just grabbed his husband's hand and dragged him into the office. Fuck the Armani suit, all Riley wanted was to be held. Josiah wasn't the problem. Crippling doubt and self-esteem issues were what made him cling to Jack. Jack smelled of the outside and horses and everything that grounded Riley.

"Josiah Harrold, Santone Corp," Jack said on a laugh. Riley pulled away.

"You know him?"

"Of him. Came courting my mom some years back when I was about fifteen. Moved on when she told him to. Before she said so he did an awful lot of tousling my hair and cooing over Beth." Jack smiled that wolfish grin—the one that Riley knew threatened mischief. "Guess I ought to follow him out and ruffle his hair?"

Riley snorted a laugh. The thought of the expression on Josiah's face if Jack's dusty working form went anywhere near him was a thought he would hold all day.

"Did he say anything to you when you passed outside?"

"Tipped his hat and said 'Campbell'."

"Did you say anything?"

"'Mornin' Josiah and it's Campbell-Hayes'," Jack said thoughtfully. "Course he may or may not have heard the extra 'asshole' I tagged on the end."

Lightness consumed Riley. Jack had this way of dragging all the shit in Riley's head down to where it could be bagged and tagged. Then a thought crossed his mind.

"Not that I don't appreciate the visit but what are you doing here in the big bad city?" CH didn't have their offices in Hayes tower but this ground floor set of linked offices was still square in the middle of the Dallas business district. Jack didn't often visit, said it gave him hives being shut in with people.

"That meeting with the trainers."

Shit. That was today?

"That was today?" Riley said. Jeez. He was so wrapped up in the oil crap that he had missed what was singularly the most important day in Jack's calendar. A consortium of riders were looking for a trainer in Texas to take on three cutting horses for training to rodeo level. "I'm sorry," Riley tagged on.

Jack simply smiled and reached up to kiss Riley full on the lips. His hands cupped Riley's face and they deepened the kiss. Riley could never get enough of this sexy length of male who plastered over him and consumed him with every touch. Wasn't married life supposed to be staid? When did they change the rule books on that one? Every day with Jack was passion and life and as a man so starved of both in his formative years, Riley drank every ounce of whatever Jack gave him. Riley melted into the kiss, took a step back toward the wall behind him, and pulled Jack along. There was no argument and Riley had a firm hold on his husband with his fingers tucked into Jack's leather belt, dragging him and holding him close.

Finally, at that point when kissing was going to either turn into one of them dropping to their knees or separating and catching their breath, Jack eased away.

"So ask me," he said. There was excitement in his expression and Riley wondered at it until his head was back in the game.

"I don't have to. They placed the horses with you, didn't they?" Riley couldn't have been happier. This was Jack's dream—to make something of the Double D and to build a future that was sustainable for Hayley.

"Yep, two weeks and we're up and running. We spent the morning at the Double D and I just dropped them at the airport."

"I'm so proud of you." Riley couldn't have said truer words. His heart was bursting with pride for Jack.

"I'll need to think about hiring some help and I need to finish off the accommodation in the new barn, and I guess I need to grab Neil and get his input. I have to—"

Riley interrupted his husband's thoughts with a kiss.

"Let's go home and talk."

Jack blinked and cast an eye around the empty office. He frowned.

"Where's Kathy?" Riley's assistant was generally in the background bustling and organizing. "And the rest of the team?"

"Kathy's daughter went into labor and she left just before the meeting finished. And the rest of the team are on site today and tomorrow. It's just me. I'll lock up and we can just go home."

"You wanna play hooky?" Jack said. He waggled his eyebrows with a leer.

"Try and stop me."

CHAPTER 5

Robbie surveyed the room with no more than a cursory glance. There was a large, solid bed, a small bath with a shower, and a closet for his clothes. That was all he wanted really.

"It's not much, being as it's over the horses but it's clean and included in the job."

"It's good." Robbie said this more for something to say than as something he thought Jack Campbell-Hayes needed to hear. They had already talked money and the big gruff cowboy was more than generous. Robbie resolved to buy Neil a huge gift as soon as his first check cleared. His friend's recommendation meant that Robbie had been the only hand that was interviewed.

"So your current horses are kept in this barn. Will we be setting out the new barn for the horses we're working with?" he asked. The second barn looked smaller but sturdy enough and he wondered why it wasn't being used. From a cursory inspection it was watertight and warm but had the general air of disuse.

"Yeah, that's kind of our barn. Mine and Riley's." Jack looked away and Robbie didn't push for more. Their barn sounded important and he wasn't going to pry.

"So the new horses, the trainers, all three of them, are in this barn?" There was definitely room for three more horses, or trainers, as they were called.

"Hence the extension when we rebuilt."

"Makes sense to have the horses together."

"So, I was thinking of offering a four-week trial," Jack explained. He leaned against the doorjamb and he looked so at ease with his thumbs hooked into his belt loops and his hat tilted forward. There was nothing except friendly welcome in Jack's eyes. That and of course the excitement that buzzed around the man. It was a big thing that these quarter horses were coming to the Double D and Jack had explained it as being the chance he needed to build a training facility here that was the best.

"That sounds more than fair. Just to be sure you know, I need to be moving on at the end of the year."

"Is there a particular reason for that time?"

"No." Robbie didn't elaborate. He had tried two stations in Australia since losing Paul but ten or so months was the most he could ever manage in one place. He didn't imagine it would be any different here. No sense in getting tied down to one place when he had the whole world to see.

They had talked the technical side. The horses, the training, the schedules, and now Robbie was being shown where he would be sleeping. The place in Australia he had shared with Paul was smaller and shabbier, not new, and far from watertight, but it had been theirs on any downtime they had. At least here on the ranch he wouldn't get homophobic idiots stomping all over him. Jack was as gay as he was, the same as his sex-on-legs husband.

"Do you have any questions for me?" Jack asked.

Robbie loved the drawl in the other man's voice—a lot more cowboy than when they had met at the wedding. He really only had one concern; one major make-or-break question that burned inside him.

"Do you ever have any trouble?"

"Trouble?" Jack frowned and then looked to be considering the question. "We sometimes get reporters at the main gate. They don't come on the land. They're only here 'cause my family and the Hayes family have been through one hell of a ton of shit and my husband Riley is freaking Dallas aristocracy."

That wasn't what Robbie meant and he wondered how he could word this. He didn't want to be anything but the best man for the job but he had to be sure.

"I meant... being gay? Does it cause problems with other people? With traders and such?"

"No." Jack straightened. "First off, we're not far outside the city—we're not in the middle of nowhere. Secondly, if I even thought anyone I had dealings with was treating me or mine with anything other than respect then they are gone."

"Okay."

"Why do you ask? Have *you* got a problem with the way I live?" Jack's friendly demeanor was edged with steel.

"No. Shit no. I... look, there's something I should have told you in the interview." Which hadn't actually been an interview, more an excited discussion about horses over coffee in Jack's kitchen with his daughter coloring at their side.

"Go on."

"The reason I left Australia and came home was because I lost my boyfriend. A couple of years ago now."

"I'm sorry—"

"When I say boyfriend I mean—" He stopped as Jack quirked an eyebrow. Robbie decided there and then that maybe he shouldn't go into an awful lot more detail.

"He was my best friend and we worked together and lived together and there was this thing... this new guy, a cowboy out of Brisbane. Didn't take too kindly to 'fags'." Robbie near spat the word and compassion passed over Jack's face. "Upshot was that Paul got in the middle and got hurt. He was knocked unconscious and he just didn't wake up."

"I am really sorry Robert—"

"Robbie, please call me Robbie."

"Robbie then. I'm not saying Texas is the safest place in the world to be out of the closet but hell, the ranch is pretty secure."

"Wyoming wasn't that good for the whole being out either."

Jack shrugged and then smiled. He changed the subject, which was probably a good thing. "So. The horses are here in just under three days and there's a whole raft of stuff we need to get done. We need to discuss incentive bonuses on training and so on, but like I said the job is yours on a four-week trial if you want it." Jack held out his hand in expectation and after only a moment's hesitation Robbie took the proffered hand and shook it firmly.

"I want it, sir."

"You want to start today?"

"Yes, sir."

"Call me Jack. Welcome to the Double D, Robbie. I'll let you get settled. Do you have to go and collect bags from anywhere?"

"Everything is in the car Neil lent me." He wasn't going to say out loud that he had cancelled his small rental a week ago and had been bunking down in a spare room over the veterinary practice. Even though Neil had offered a room in the large building to the side of the practice, Robbie really didn't want to outstay his welcome with his newly married best friend. If the interview today had gone badly then he had resolved to find a motel somewhere to sleep tonight before moving on. Perhaps up north to find a spread he could work on. Now, it seemed with the interview going well that he would have his own place.

"Bring your gear up, take some time to get yourself settled. Starting tomorrow is soon enough. Dinner's in the main house at seven and I can give you keys to this place."

* * * * *

Robbie knocked on the door and waited. He wasn't entirely sure what the protocol was here. Back on the station he had been one of twenty-six hands and there was a separate bunkhouse complex with a cook. Jack hadn't mentioned any other staff; it would seem apart from Jack and him there was only Riley and their daughter. There was a small area in his room with a burner and a sink, a small fridge, and a toaster oven. He would be more than happy to keep himself fed. Being at the owners' table was always difficult. He would have to be polite and mind his manners and after a hard day out on horseback that was sometimes hard to do. They in turn would have to be polite back, and act like they were happy to have a hired hand at their table. It was a lose-lose situation. Just tonight then probably. A 'welcome to the ranch' dinner. A shower, clean jeans, and a shave had been the right thing to do.

The door flew open like someone had yanked at it from the other side and suddenly Robbie was face-to-face with a laughing Riley.

"Come in," he said. Leaving the door, he disappeared and after a few moments' consideration of whether he could keep his boots on with a tiled floor he followed where Riley had gone. Straight into the kitchen and slap-bang in the middle of chaos. Hayley was on a chair helping Jack with something at the sink and Riley had joined them.

"We need more carrots," Riley said.

"And broccoli," Hayley added.

"More meat," Jack insisted.

"We don't need more meat. It's not good for you, Pappa," Hayley remonstrated. Robbie bit back a laugh. How often had his mamma told him he needed to eat less meat and more greens.

"Help me, Robbie," Jack pleaded. "My fellow cowboy, tell me you eat meat with every meal."

"Sure do, sir… Jack."

"Jack has this saying," Riley started. "That if he had to take a pill…" Riley paused and then between laughs he and Hayley singsonged the remainder of the sentence, *"'I'd wrap it in bacon first'."*

Jack shrugged and then Robbie saw him exchanging a broad grin with Riley.

"Well it's two-all now. So you can keep your greens on your plate and give all the meat to me and Robbie. Agreed, Robbie?"

Jack was talking to him. Asking him something that implied Robbie would be spending more dinners in this worn and cozy kitchen. He wasn't entirely sure how he felt about that.

"Agreed," he said.

Hayley clambered down and under the watchful eye of both Riley and Jack she came to a stop in front of Robbie who wasn't rightly sure he knew where to stand.

"Come sit down with me," she ordered. She settled into what he supposed was her seat at the large scarred and worn table. When they were both sitting she held out a hand. "Hayley Samuels," she said.

He shook her small hand.

"Robbie Curtis. We met at the wedding, didn't we?" Robbie asked.

"We did," Hayley answered. "It's Daddy's turn to cook tonight but Pappa always says there isn't enough meat in the stuff he makes."

"He does?" What else did you say to a slip of a girl with shiny eyes and the confidence of a kid much older than she looked.

When the men appeared finished with whatever they were cooking, some kind of meat in one pot with potatoes thing, they took chairs at the same table and Jack handed Robbie a beer. They passed the time with talk about the ranch and covered Riley's aims for his exploration company as Robbie listened and learned. These two men had something he had never experienced before. A love so deep that you could see it. In every gesture or touch or word Jack and Riley were what Robbie wished for and had never found. They were happy.

"Tell him what you do." Jack sounded so damned proud and Robbie waited expectantly for Riley to explain.

"I have a small team working on the auctions for exploration rights of undersea minerals in the western Gulf of Mexico. It's a fledgling consultancy and it deals mostly with ethical exploration for oil." Riley spoke as if he had rehearsed it and he said it all while clutching Jack's hand. That was interesting to see. Robbie guessed from that action that Riley needed Jack's support. Jack simply listened and nodded. They were good together. When Jack talked about his quarter horses it had been Riley this and Riley that. *Interesting.*

"Can you cook?" Jack asked Robbie as the three men and Hayley cleared the huge crockpot of beef stew.

"I like to cook," Robbie answered. In fact he *loved* to cook but he didn't often get the chance. Either that or he was so engrossed in his job that he'd forget to eat let alone cook. He was ready to cook in his small kitchenette area but it wasn't the same as what he could create if he had a chance in this kitchen.

"Tell me I can add you to the rotation then?" Jack pleaded.

"Rotation?"

"We have a rotation for cooking and since you'll be eating here—"

"Maybe you should ask if he wants to eat with us?" Riley interrupted.

"Do you? Want to eat here with the family?"

Robbie didn't hesitate. He imagined other nights wouldn't be as laid back as tonight, and that there could sometimes be a lot of different tensions at play. There always was in any household. But he felt comfortable here.

"Of course. And I'll take my turn on the rotation."

"Can you cook chicken?" Hayley asked around a mouthful of potato. "'Cause Pappa can't and it tastes bad. Daddy burns it all the time."

"Fried chicken you mean?" Robbie asked. Hayley nodded vigorously. "One of my favorite dishes."

"Consider yourself rotation-ed," Jack said.

"What is Australia like? Is that where you learned to cook?" Hayley asked.

They had finished dinner and Robbie was just considering whether he should be leaving the kitchen and making his way back to his room. The question threw him. To start explaining would mean quite a bit longer sat at the table. Jack pushed a mug of coffee his way and lifted an eyebrow. Clearly he wanted to know as well.

Robbie began.

* * * * *

Riley excused himself and made his way to the small office area he and Jack shared. Moving aside the new copy of *Quarter Horse Monthly* he started his laptop and signed in. There were five e-mails, three of which he forwarded straight to Kathy for dealing with at a much later date—

speculative e-mails that offered deals of a lifetime. Kathy was the expert at weeding those out.

An especially loud burst of laughter came from the kitchen and Riley smiled. It was good to hear Jack laughing and finally finding someone he felt comfortable with. Hayley walked into the room and climbed on his knee.

"I'm going to bed," she said. She hugged him close and he held tight to her in return. There was no school tomorrow so Hayley was using the agreed extra hour of wakefulness to her advantage. She was planning a day out with friends from school but Riley pushed down any worries he had whenever she was out of his sight. She was nine now, ten in September, and she needed friends and a life away from the ranch. School was good and it was more than Riley had ever experienced. It had been one tutor after another and he'd only really made friends, people like Eli, when he was at college. Even then they were friends made in an alcoholic, sexaholic haze. No wonder he never kept up with Eli after his friend had been 'encouraged' to leave the college.

"Robbie is gonna cook chicken tomorrow and you hafta make sure you pick me up in time from Sophie's."

"I will."

"Promise, Daddy?"

"I promise."

"I love you."

"I love you too, baby."

"Night." She kissed him on the cheek and cuddled closer. A quiet time like this when he could hold the miracle that was his daughter was very special to Riley.

That random thought about a brother or sister for her filtered into his head. Gay couples all over were expanding their families one way or another. Surrogacy or adoption—either was a valid route. The idea of a baby on the ranch? Beth's baby had been fine here, she and Steve and the baby often visited, and Emily was walking now, under a watchful eye, around the fences and the horses even at her young age. Yet again Riley filed the thought away for one day talking to Jack. One day.

Hayley climbed down and disappeared out of the door with a wave. Riley would go in and check on her later. Make sure she had brushed her teeth, see if she had braided her long blonde hair, the usual daddy stuff. Then he would tell her he loved her again and she would tell him back.

The little things he cherished the most about being with his daughter made this one of the perfect times of the day.

CHAPTER 6

Jack woke before dawn had even lightened the room. Today was the day that the three horses were being delivered for training. He knew he had slept maybe an hour out of the whole night and he knew why. He was scared and nervous all wrapped into one. This was a huge responsibility. He was being paid to do what he loved but with the added pressure of having to do it right. The owners expected way more than Jack had ever had to fulfill with his own horses. Solo-Cal and her offspring were bred for covering, not for action in the ring or the field. He only hoped he was good enough.

He eased himself out from under Riley, who had this habit of using his long arms to completely encompass Jack. Something Jack loved but that made it difficult to get up without Riley reacting and waking up. Gently he completed the extrication and sat on the edge of the bed. The room was cool outside of the covers and he could feel the hairs on his arms prickle and rise. Goose bumps at ass o'clock in the morning was one way to ensure he stayed awake for the duration.

"Stop worrying," Riley said. His voice was sleepy but firm. *Great.* Clearly his escapology act had actually woken Riley up.

"I can't."

"Come here." Riley pushed a hand under him and almost levered him from where he was to half lie over Riley. Jack wanted to relax badly but so many emotions warred inside him. Inhaling the Riley's scent, he forced himself to relax.

"I love you," he whispered. Riley wriggled a bit closer and his heat was a furnace but he was already dropping back to sleep and said nothing in return. He didn't need to. Jack knew how Riley felt.

Neil would be here in a little over three hours. Maybe if Jack pushed himself and relaxed every single muscle then he could sleep. Matching his breathing to Riley's he thought happy thoughts of Hayley and horses. His thoughts hooked on Hayley and the tiny scrap of girl that was so much a miniature Riley. He wondered what a daughter with his genes would look like. Would she have his blue eyes? Would she love horses like he did? What if it was a boy? What if they had a boy?

He slept.

* * * * *

Neil looked very official in a shirt and suit and he stood next to Jack with an air of confidence about him. Jack wished he felt as confident.

"They're taking a big chance on me," he confided. They watched as the horse transports approached and the tension inside Jack was now knotted beyond comfort.

"No, they're not. They know horses, you know horses." Neil made it sound so simple. Jack glanced at his whatever-relation-he-was-officially-kind-of-a-friend guy. He wished he had the same confidence today. This was such an odd feeling to be experiencing. He knew what he was doing, so why was he so damn nervous?

"Boss. Neil," Robbie said as he joined them.

Jack looked over at his hand who was bright-eyed and bushy-tailed and had probably had way more sleep than he had. Robbie had been a godsend. A hard worker and cheerfully confident in what he did, he had organized the stables for today, and Jack approved of everything he had done. So what if he had caught the guy staring at Riley. What gay man in his right mind wouldn't want to stare at Riley. Riley was beautiful, sexy, and fucking hot. He would be surprised if any sane gay man didn't at least want a taste of what Riley could offer. *God. I'm tired*, he thought. *Robbie does not want in my husband's pants.* Still, it wouldn't hurt to keep an eye on that. *I will not let jealousy get in the way of today.*

"You okay, boss?" Robbie asked.

Yeah, I worry you stare at my husband and I know Riley likes cowboys. Like he was going to say that. He was being freaking irrational.

"Just tired and if I'm honest, nervous."

"Nothing to be nervous about," Robbie said. "You know your shit."

Jack smiled at the simple statement. Between him and Robbie and Neil they could do this thing. They could expand the Double D. They could.

The trucks pulled up, one, two, three, in front of them. Each driver left room at the rear to offload the animals and finally the time for stepping up to the plate was here.

"Let's do this thing," Jack said.

The morning passed in a flurry of activity until finally three horses for training were in their respective stables waiting on Neil's assessment while Jack signed paperwork and did what he hated—schmoozed the owners. When Neil countersigned as chief veterinarian contact they left until finally it was Jack, Neil, and Robbie leaning on the stall doors and talking.

"All three are fine animals," Neil noted.

"They are," Robbie agreed.

"So we'll start tomorrow?" Jack said.

"In my experience the transfer will cause a few issues, so yeah, but gentle stuff," Robbie commented.

"Agreed." What Robbie said made sense. Out of the three, Daisy, Storm, and Catty, only Daisy was restless and irritable. The other two were calm and still. Jack climbed the stable door and stood by Daisy, just talking low and gentle. The scent of the horse was reassuring and he murmured soft words.

"It'll be fine little lady… you'll like it here…" On and on he chatted and stroked and settled the feisty roan. Alex brayed a disapproving warning from her stall. She'd probably be put out that Jack was spending time with new horses. His girls were possessive and loving. Out of the corner of his eye he saw Robbie join Alex in the stall on the other side and when Alex finally settled Jack knew one thing.

He had found the right man in Robbie.

CHAPTER 7

Riley might have known Josiah wouldn't let things rest. Even after contracts were finalized he was causing trouble and the latest press release from Santone Corp was absolutely perfect evidence of that.

He was pacing and didn't stop even when Eli walked into his office and stared in amusement.

"What's wrong?" his friend asked.

"Nothing," Riley snapped.

"Okay."

"Shit. Fuck. Why would he do this?"

Eli stopped Riley's pacing only by physically standing in his way and when they collided it was enough to snap Riley out of his anger.

"Start from the beginning?"

"It doesn't matter. One of the partners in this deal has issued a press release and it got my back up more than you can think."

"What did it say?"

"Long story short, he's come over all 'I'm guiding the young Riley Hayes, son of Gerald Hayes, to stop him from making mistakes like his daddy'." Riley looked to Eli for a reaction. Eli had never actually met Gerald Hayes but Riley had told him enough to give his friend the idea that they didn't get on.

"Who's printed it?"

"Everyone."

"What does it mean for you? Will it undermine what you've done, or is it just embarrassing shit? Or can you just ignore it until it is yesterday's news?"

Riley sighed. This was just Josiah taking a pop at him in the hope of stirring something. All the anger and need to smack something disintegrated in a second and he perched on the edge of his desk.

"You're right."

"I am?"

"It's just embarrassing. And fuck, they didn't even get my surname right."

"Okay. So here's what you do. Contact the big presses with a release. Something about how you love learning from the old guys so you can see what you could do differently."

"That would be childish," Riley said.

"Damn right it would. Doesn't mean you have to do it… but you know you could."

"Since when did you get so wise, Eli? As I remember it, your advice at college was confined to sexual positions, pranks, and kinds of beer." Riley was joking but something twinged inside him when Eli's answering grin dimmed a little. Riley watched as his friend caught himself and replaced the nervous, thin-lipped smile with his trademark grin again. Something in Eli's eyes, a flicker of pain, of hurt, and Riley wanted Eli to know he was here for him. How did he even say that when all he was working on was instinct?

"Shit happens," Eli quipped. "You promised me lunch?"

Riley grabbed his phone and led the way out of his office, passing Kathy with a nod and a "be back later". They walked a short distance from the office until they found a café and both ordered chicken salad. Hot days called for ice water and a beer.

"You never said what you were up to when you decided to leave college."

"You mean when I was kicked out?"

"You did crash the dean's car."

"It was an accident." Eli looked so damned serious but then his face broke into a grin. "Nice car. Shame it was totaled. Dad replaced it but it was the first in a long list of life lessons. Now you see me"—he gestured down at himself—"all responsible and grown up."

"I was sorry to hear about your dad."

"Ten for drug dealing you mean?" Eli wasn't expecting a response and Riley simply nodded. "Apparently he'd blown his inheritance, hence he's blown mine, blah blah, etcetera, and so on. We don't talk. In fact we stopped talking when I, in his words, *decided* to be gay when I was sixteen. Then we moved on to a simple financial relationship. Not nice."

"I remember you said that."

"I did?" Eli looked surprised. Clearly he didn't share that story around.

"You were drunk at the time."

"That explains my lack of discretion then. Of course it didn't help that Mom did the whole Playboy MILF spread." Eli shook his head in disbelief at what he was saying. Riley imagined his friend was still reeling from that one as well. "Then there was the cancer."

Riley was busy looking at the approaching waiter with their food and his arrival broke into the conversation. As soon as the guy left Riley simply ignored his food and looked at Eli. Cancer? He hadn't heard that right. Surely not Eli?

"Cancer? Your mom? Dad?"

Eli twisted his mouth in a parody of a smile then tapped his side. "No, me. In my kidney. It's rare for people under forty to get kidney cancer but leave it to me to be the one in a million. Had the diagnosis maybe a few months after I left college, moved back home, had the treatment. Instead of taking out all of the kidney, the surgeon just removed the tumor and the part of the kidney surrounding it. Lost my hair though with the chemo." He tapped his head. The hair there was thick and tamed and Riley couldn't actually picture Eli without hair.

"Shit. I'm sorry." Riley sat back in his seat, deflated.

Eli shrugged.

"It's done with now. The meds I was on made me tired and I hated that. I was trapped inside for such a long time. So when I was better, a few years back I suppose, I took my camera and left the house to get some air. Haven't looked back."

Riley extended his arm to touch Eli but hesitated. Eli may not want sympathy. Instead Eli grabbed his hand and held it. They gripped hands across the table and Riley felt regret swell inside him that he hadn't been there for his friend.

"Can it come back?" Riley asked.

Eli shook his head. "It can but I don't think about it. It's been a few years and everything is clear so far."

After releasing their mutual grip, Eli forked a huge pile of salad into his mouth and treated Riley to a view of mashed pasta and sauce on his tongue.

Riley sighed. "You'll never grow up, will you."

Eli swallowed. "Nope."

Riley couldn't even begin to think about what he had just said. Eli was the same age as Riley, only a couple of months separated his July birthday from Eli's in September.

"I'm sorry, you know, for what happened at college," Riley offered finally. Might as well deal with the elephant in the room.

"You mean for that argument?" Eli pushed pasta to one side of his plate and then looked up directly at Riley.

"It was stupid and I've grown up a lot since then." Riley said this knowing it to be true. "I slept around with so many different people you were right to call me on it."

"Nah, I was just a kid who was jealous that you could sleep with all those different people. Anyway, how can I be angry for anything you did with anyone at college, including Lexie, when you have Hayley to show for it?"

Riley smiled at the mention of his daughter. The he sobered.

"If we hadn't argued I could have been there for you when you were ill." The words hung there. They had been good friends pushed apart by Eli trying to do the right thing and rein in Riley's catting around, and he couldn't regret his stupid reaction enough. "You wouldn't have got drunk and taken the car."

Both men sat quietly for a moment, each remembering the dean's car in the lake and the subsequent sending away of one Eli drunk-off-his-ass Martin. Eli laughed first. When Riley got past the whole thing of not believing Eli was laughing about what had happened, he joined in. Seeing his friend sitting on the bank watching over a hundred thousand dollars of Ferrari ass end up in lake mud was pretty fucking hysterical. Argument or not, Eli had certainly left the college with a bang.

"Tell me about this arranged marriage thing then," Eli asked. He had stopped laughing and the waiter had cleared the plates.

Riley took the opener for what it was—the chance for Eli to change the subject—and using as many funny stories as he could he gave Eli the whitewashed version of how he had met Jack and how he had fallen in love.

With a whole lot more laughing and no thinking the bad things that had happened to death.

That was a new experience for Riley.

* * * * *

"Jeez. What did you say when he told you?" Jack asked. Eli had cancer? That wasn't what Jack had expected as the outcome of his husband meeting Eli for lunch.

"I didn't say anything. What could I say? He trusted me with the news and I think he wanted me to just go with the flow. So we did. We talked a lot about you. I think he has a small crush on you. We just carried on like it's every day someone you know lays having cancer on you."

"Cancer is harsh," Jack commented.

"The way Eli explained it made it all sound so simple. But it seemed as we chatted that Eli was alone when it happened. He was out of college and not in touch with friends, not in touch with me, and with his mom and dad who didn't give much of a shit about anything but themselves." Riley sounded alternately sad and remorseful. "If I'd known—"

"He didn't tell you. How could you have known?" Jack tried to be the sensible one.

"I never should have been such a child over Lexie. He told me I was treating her like shit, cheating on her, and we argued."

Jesus, Riley was so hard on himself. Why did he do that? What purpose did it serve to beat himself up over not being there for a friend so many years ago.

"I know. You said when he first visited," Jack commented in summary.

"I was a dickhead."

"Riley." Jack said the single word with a note of warning and Riley subsided to looking into his coffee cup morosely. Sometimes all Riley needed was to be told not to think a certain way. Not that Jack assumed it immediately impacted his husband to stop worrying. It did, however, reset Riley's worry so that he could break the cycle of beating himself up over things. Amazing how much you learned about people in a few years. Like Riley knew that standing in Jack's way had the effect that Jack's temper went from boiling to merely simmering. Words wouldn't stop the temper but Riley physically blocking Jack always did.

Jack's cell rang and he scrambled to reach it before the requisite four rings took it to voicemail. He'd been expecting a call from Neil about Daisy, who was really unsettled despite this being the second week since she arrived.

"Hello?" He answered quickly. He hadn't even looked at the screen. He listened for a few minutes and watched as Riley was checking his cell phone for messages, the tall man slouching so he could lean on the side counter.

"Mr Campbell-Hayes, I'm so pleased to reach you directly. My name is Frank Templeton and I am on the committee for the Texas Gay Rodeo Association. Maybe you have heard of us?"

"I have. How can I help?"

"Mr Campbell-Hayes, we have a proposition for you."

Jack listened. He heard every word that Frank Templeton said, but he wasn't sure they had the right man. He didn't say as much; he didn't want to seem rude. Best take the offer at face value he guessed.

"Thank you," he said. "It's an honor to be asked. I will have an answer to you by tomorrow."

Frank ended the call and Jack stared at his phone in bewilderment. He couldn't believe what he had just been asked and he sat at the kitchen table with his coffee and a completely blank hole where his thought processes should have been.

"Who was it?"

Pause.

"Jack?"

Pause.

"Talk to me... what's wrong? Is it Beth?"

Riley was talking to him and Jack blinked away the shock. "No, not Beth. That was a guy from the TGRA; they want me to be a judge with the gay rodeo that's holding finals in Texas in October." He finally managed to get the words out and then slumped in his seat.

"TGRA?"

"Texas Gay Rodeo Association."

"A judge."

"Uh huh."

"Well that's cool, I've seen you on a horse and you're good. You know what you're looking for."

"I haven't been to a rodeo in a couple years," Jack muttered. Since meeting Riley, and working at the Double D, and then all the stuff with Hayley, he just hadn't had time. Stupid really, because training the quarter horses was what he was good at and he was cutting himself off from the very market that wanted him. He was lucky that so far he had managed a good living on word of mouth but he really should be out there marketing himself.

"I've never been to a rodeo," Riley answered. He sounded wistful.

"It's a *gay* rodeo." There was so much emphasis on the word gay that Riley laughed and Jack just scowled at the reaction. Riley evidently couldn't resist his scowly face and he scooted closer so he could hold Jack's hand.

"Then we should feel right at home," Riley said.

Jack wasn't feeling that. He had very specific ideas of what being gay meant to him. He was a cowboy and gay and goddamn proud of both. That didn't mean he had to go around proclaiming it to all and everyone. He should just go to a normal straight rodeo.

"I don't know what I'm going to say to them."

"Yes you do. You'll say yes. They're doing good work. It's not easy being a gay cowboy; hell, it's not all that easy being gay."

Jack narrowed his eyes. Riley was awfully behind this for some reason and Jack was suddenly very suspicious. "Did you know about this?"

"No," Riley answered, far too quickly. Jack stood and Riley followed just as quickly and in a few steps he had a laughing Riley pressed back against the kitchen wall.

"Tell me—"

"No." Riley laughed.

Jack could work this one of two ways. He could finesse the information he needed out of Riley over the space of two days or he could go for the kill now, using sex.

Pressing himself close he could feel Riley was already hard and Jack was enjoying this so much he wasn't far behind. Whether Riley had something to do with this or not could wait for just a little while. They kissed with all the sensual abandon of a committed couple, lust mixed with love. The embrace heated and Jack set up a rocking rhythm. He knew Hayley was in her room and could walk in on them, but he knew equally well that the kitchen door was shut and stuck like a bastard. He would hear her coming. God help anyone who came in the front door as they were likely to get an eyeful any second now. Riley was limp beneath him, held up by Jack's body and the firm hold Jack had on Riley's hands. He pulled back.

"I'm going to drop to my knees and suck your brains out of your dick," Jack said. Talking sexy never had really amounted to any more than telling Riley exactly what he wanted to do to him. Talking pretty was okay for some but Riley said he loved this about Jack so that was what Riley was going to get.

"Guh," Riley moaned. The single non-word was Riley's only reply as he thumped his head back on the wall and pushed his groin into Jack's.

"Then I'm going to drape you over this table and fuck you into tomorrow. Make love to you so damn good that you're gonna see stars—"

"Jack. Please—"

"After…" Jack deliberately trailed off in what he was saying.

"After?" Riley prompted in a husky, low voice.

"After you tell me what you know about this rodeo." Jack stepped back and Riley near stumbled. He was limp as a noodle and Jack could see the surprise in his husband's eyes.

"Blow job first?" Riley pleaded. He reached for Jack but Jack took a step away and smiled his 'no'. It was torture standing this close to six-four of muscled, excited husband when all he wanted to do was drop to his knees and show Riley a good time.

"Damn it, Jack. They called last week when you were out with the horses so I knew they were calling back. Anyways, I think it would be good marketing for the Double D."

"Okay," Jack said. That made sense. Whatever else concerned Jack, the ranch was at the forefront of everything he decided. That, and Riley, and Hayley, and his family, oh, and his friends. Okay, so it was a long-assed list.

"Okay?" Riley looked surprised that Jack was leaving it at that.

But Jack knew something Riley didn't. Jack really wanted his mouth on Riley's dick. Dropping to his knees, he scooted forward until his lips touched denim-covered hardness. He heard Riley inhale and the two of them fumbled to open buttons and to pull denim and cotton down enough to expose Riley. Jack didn't tease, or lick, or anything he might usually do. He wanted to make love to Riley the rest of the goddamned night. He closed his lips around Riley and sucked him down and Riley near whimpered above him.

"Jesus, fuck," Riley groaned. Jack knew his husband's body so well, was well versed in every single inch of Riley and the points that sent him wild. "I'm going to come too fast—Jack—Jeez..."

With Jack's hands reaching and touching and kneading Riley's ass, Riley lost it after what seemed like no time at all and Jack didn't waste any of time. Climbing Riley's body, he ravaged his husband's mouth with a kiss, sharing the taste of him. He dragged him away from the kitchen and to their bedroom where he pushed Riley down on the bed. Riley was bigger, taller, wider, but he wasn't fighting this. Jack spent a moment just staring at the length of Riley spread out over their bed. An overwhelming wave of love consumed Jack and suddenly all thoughts of just taking Riley here and now were gone. Sometimes they took and stole and lost themselves in each other. Tonight Jack wanted more. He wanted slow. He pressed down on his erection and started to undress. Riley followed suit.

Jack climbed on the bed.

"What's wrong?" Riley asked gently.

"Nothing," Jack replied. He was worrying at Riley's right nipple, kissing and gently biting. Riley arched up into the touch and Jack let him. "I love you," he whispered onto heated skin.

"I love you too," Riley said.

The heat from the day was dissipating but the room was still warm. For a second Jack rested his forehead on Riley's chest. The rodeo call was one thing but it paled next to how he felt about the news that Eli had been ill.

Eli was so alive and real, just like Riley. If Jack lost Riley now, if he had to face a future without his husband, he wasn't sure how long he could go on. He would have to, he was named as guardian for Hayley, but to live in a world without Riley? How could he even start to imagine that?

"I'm so sorry for Eli," he said. His voice was muffled against Riley but his husband heard him. Riley eased him up until Jack was lying next to him.

"Me too," he admitted. "He'll be okay. He's got this whole 'getting out there and doing things now' kind of attitude. I actually feel sorry for anyone who gets in his way."

Talking turned to kissing and when they began to make love it was slow and long and so full of love that Jack was choked.

He kissed a path from lips to chest again. The two cinnamon discs on Riley's chest were two of Jack's favorite things, along with Riley's height, his hair, his eyes, the taste of him, his legs, ass, back, shoulders… hell, everything. The cool evening breeze moved the thin net curtains at the window. Riley reached into the top drawer of the small bedside table and pulled out lube. The pure intimacy with which Riley moved when Jack was stretching him was never as exquisite as the sounds he made when Jack took him.

"Now," Riley murmured. Jack took no notice; he was running this show, and he wanted slow and steady even as he pushed his way in and kissed the wince of burn from Riley's lips.

"Shhh," he whispered. "I'll get you there." Curling himself around Riley, fingers tracing each muscle and the taut cords of his neck, Jack buried himself again and again. Every push was accompanied by whispers of encouragement and Riley was cursing and writhing on Jack's dick until finally he came with a shout muffled by Jack's kiss.

Jack felt that he would have to be superhuman not to have come as soon as he entered Riley but somehow Jack had managed to make it last. He pushed deep inside one final time and came hard in Riley. Replete and exhausted Jack managed to stumble to the bathroom and find a cloth and, finally cleaned, he checked in on Hayley and then they both slumped back onto the bed. The humidity in the room was too much to be under the covers.

"Do you still want dinner?" Jack asked.

"Too tired," Riley replied.

"It's only nine."

"You wore me out." Riley moved his face against the cool pillows and suddenly all Jack wanted to do was lie here next to his husband.

"Did you lock up?" Riley asked. His voice sounded sleepy.

"Uh huh," Jack replied, "When I checked on Hayley."

"Hayley's okay?"

"Fast asleep."

Riley snuggled in close and Jack wrapped his arms around him.

Nothing was taking Riley from him. Not another man, or woman, or cancer, or anything.

Ever.

CHAPTER 8

Robbie paused inside the open door. The man that was standing in the kitchen with his fingers dancing over a phone was not Jack, nor Riley. The air was redolent with the smell of cooking and a quick glance to the sink showed a pile of peelings that indicated the meal included potatoes at least.

"Hi," Robbie said. The other guy was turned half away from him and clearly hadn't heard him come into the kitchen. He also apparently hadn't heard Robbie say hi. Either that or he was terminally rude.

"No. I don't want him again," other-guy snapped. For a second Robbie was startled at the vehemence in the man's voice then just as quickly realized he had earbuds in and was clearly talking on his phone. "Because last time he stripped naked, waggled his dick in my face, and asked me to call him sir." Robbie couldn't help the raising of his eyebrows at that statement. "Then I caught him oiling up Harvey in the back room. No. Okay. Find me someone else." With a heavy sigh he finished the call and pulled the earbuds from his ears. "Fuck," he muttered.

"Hi," Robbie tried again. The guy jumped a foot in the air and whirled to face Robbie.

"Shit!" He grasped at his chest dramatically and his eyes were wide with shock. "You scared the fuck out of me."

"Sorry," Robbie apologized. He watched as the guy waved away the apology with a grin.

"It's cool. I needed snapping out of my oncoming temper tantrum." He extended his hand in welcome. "Eli Martin, friend of Riley's."

Robbie took the hand and shook it. "Robbie. I work here."

Eli cast an appraising look up and then deliberately down the full length of Robbie, all while he gripped Robbie's hand.

"I bet you do," he near purred.

Robbie became a little concerned, pulled his hand away, and pushed it deep into his pocket. He was ignoring the firm grasp and the slide of skin on skin like he had imagined it all. Eli was still staring. For a second Robbie wondered if he had nicked himself shaving or something, so intently was Eli examining his face. When Jack had muttered about having a guest for dinner Robbie had made an effort because he didn't know who it was. He had showered, shaved, and dressed in his best jeans, the ones from the wedding, before pulling on a clean pale blue T-shirt. Hell, he'd even tried to tame his unruly hat hair with gel that Paul had bought him three years before. Of course he'd had to scrape away the crusty end of the tube but the gel was still sticky and his sun-bleached blond hair took on a tousled, wild appearance.

He wasn't sure where to look and was now moving way past uncomfortable to downright verging on pissed. The gaze of Eli's green eyes—his deep mossy eyes with amber flecks—was so focused that the inspection seared through Robbie. Instead of returning the gaze Robbie focused straight ahead on Eli's short, spiky dark hair.

"You're a cowboy?" Eli asked finally.

Robbie wasn't sure where to place the tone in Eli's voice. He sounded almost excited and at the same time disbelieving.

"Yes," Robbie answered. He took a step back and away from the guy who would not quit with the freaky staring.

"Have you ever thought of modeling?"

The question was so far out of left field that Robbie was momentarily speechless. In all of his near thirty years he had never been handed that particular inquiry. Robbie stared directly into green eyes and swallowed. Eli was vibrating with visible tension and he really wasn't sure what the hell was going on.

"Leave Robbie alone."

Robbie was never more grateful when Jack, followed by Riley and Hayley, entered the kitchen.

"But he's so pretty and I wasn't touching," Eli whined.

Robbie was damn sure he had never been called pretty before. Hot. Hard. Sexy. Never pretty. Not that he believed much of what he was told. Besides, Eli was the pretty one. Shorter than him, he had full lips and the longest eyelashes. Eli was all city; polished and urbane, and Robbie couldn't help himself and dropped his gaze to Eli's crotch to admire the way his pants were pulled by his groin. Jack moved between Robbie and Eli and quirked his lips in a wry smile.

"Sorry. Ignore Eli."

"Most people do," Riley added.

The table was already laid for five and within the space of ten minutes or so dinner was served. Eli didn't stop looking at him and every time Robbie couldn't help but look back Eli was sizing him up and smiling. Unnerving.

Unsettling. Kinda hot. Eli was nothing like Paul. Paul had been taller, wider, a cowboy, at home in denim and dust. Eli was like some kind of weird ranch version of a businessman. He wore pants not jeans, a button-down shirt not a T-shirt, and his hair was short and spiky and probably gelled with product that was newer than three years old.

He discovered that talking to Hayley formed a useful barrier between him and Eli, who really would not quit with the staring. At nine, with dinner cleared away, Robbie was so freaked out that he nearly dived out the door to leave.

"Coffee?" Jack asked.

"No thank you. Dinner was great," Robbie said. "I'm turning in. Night." Nodding to Jack and Riley and with a small movement to include Eli and no further backward glance he was gone out of the door. He pulled it shut behind him only to have the whole thing move as apparently Eli had chosen to follow him out.

Robbie didn't wait. With long strides he made his way over the ground to the barn. The half dusk made it difficult to see but he was used to uneven ground and made it to the steps up the side of the barn with little difficulty.

"Wait. Robbie—fuck!" The fuck was accompanied by a rather loud thud and was followed up by a ripe curse that split the evening air. Robbie paused with his foot on the bottom step. He had made it so close to his actual room; almost got all the way to safety and now his innate sense of chivalry made him turn around. Sprawled in the dust, Eli was prone and not moving. Robbie had heard him curse so he assumed the guy was still alive—he was probably just winded. That was all. Any minute now he would roll to his side and stand. He didn't.

"Jeez," Robbie sighed. Striding back the few steps to where Eli lay, he wondered if maybe he should press the guy's side with his toe. Or find a stick.

"Ouch," Eli muttered.

Well, at least the man was alive. That was a good thing. Right?

"What the hell are you doing?" Robbie asked. Impatience colored the question.

"What the fuck does it look like I'm doing?" Eli sounded pissed, as well he should.

"It looks like you're sprawled in the dirt in your fancy clothes with shit all over you."

Eli experimentally sniffed the air. "I landed in shit?"

"No, Eli, you didn't land in shit. That was a euphemism for landing on your ass on cowboy land."

Eli raised his eyebrows. Perhaps he wasn't expecting long words from a cowboy? He held up a hand. "Help me up? Please?" He added the please when Robbie took a step back and away. Robbie's manners and his sense of duty warred with his common sense. This was Riley's friend sprawled on the ground. He couldn't leave him there. Could he? Eli made him feel all kinds of uncomfortable and hot and jeez, did he mention uncomfortable.

"Is he okay?" Riley was calling from the door. Evidently the whole thing had been caught out of the kitchen window.

"Are you okay?" Robbie snapped the question.

"Help me up." Eli sounded a little pitiful and Robbie wondered if the guy had actually hurt himself.

Robbie sighed and then did as he was asked. He held out a hand and leaned down. Eli grasped tightly and scrambled to stand. Momentarily Robbie was off balance but flexing the muscles in his arms he managed to pull Eli close enough not to end up face planted in the dirt himself.

"I'm fine, Ri," Eli called to the waiting Riley. "Robbie has me."

"Eli…" Riley's voice held warning but Eli just turned back to face Robbie even as he spoke firmly to Riley.

"I just want to talk."

Robbie sighed as his simmering irritability morphed into the start of anger.

"Talking would involve actual words," he said. He tried to keep his voice low enough so Riley wouldn't hear him. "Not sitting opposite me with your mouth hanging open and your eyes on my dick."

"Are you going to let go of me, cowboy?" Eli said gently.

Robbie cursed when he realized he still had hold of the photographer and released him as quickly as he could without letting the guy tumble back again. Robbie heard the screen door shutting and assumed Riley was back in the house. Damn. There went the cavalry. Hell, he needed to be handling this himself—he couldn't go running to Jack complaining that Riley's friend made him feel like a bug under a microscope.

"There," Robbie said. Perhaps a little unnecessarily but he wanted to draw a line of emphasis under the whole incident. Finished.

"Can we talk?"

"What about?" Robbie couldn't keep the suspicion out of his voice. "I'm not a model or a clotheshorse or whatever shit you think you see in me."

Eli lifted a hand and touched Robbie's cheek. He stepped back startled. Not even Paul had touched him in such an intimate and gentle way. That wasn't the way things worked.

"What the hell!" he snapped.

"I have twenty models arriving in a few days and not one of them is as perfect as you. Your cheekbones, jeez, you could cut stone with them, and your eyes. Did you know your eyes are the most peculiar shade of blue? Like a sky just before a storm, all dark and brooding."

"I'm going to bed." Robbie had really had enough of all this crap tonight. He resolved to never have anything to do with Eli ever again. He even turned to go but Eli's soft "wait" made him stop. Irritated, he turned on his heel.

"What?"

"I like you."

"You *like* me? You don't *know* me."

"I want to—"

"Jeez—"

"Look. Wait. That isn't me being creepy." Eli looked so intense when he said that and with the light from the house spilling into their corner of darkness Robbie could see real emotion on the other man's face. "This is me wanting something artistically. I mean, shit, I'm a photographer—"

"I know—"

"And I am inspired by you—"

"Whatever—"

"I would give anything to shoot you on film."

"No."

"Then this is me also thinking you are kind of cool. The stories you must have about your time in the outback. I would love to hear more when I am taking your photo about then and the kangaroos."

"Kangaroos?" Robbie couldn't have stopped the snort of laughter if he'd tried.

"Yes. In Australia. Y'know, kangaroos." Eli lifted his hands in front of him in an approximation of kangaroo front paws and even hopped up on his toes before catching himself.

"I know what a kangaroo is." Robbie shook his head.

"So would you think about it?"

"I already did. No. I'm not having my photo plastered everywhere for people to look at—"

"It would just be for me," Eli interrupted.

Robbie wasn't sure what to say to that one.

"That's not leveling out the creepiness factor here."

"I'd pay you." Eli was clearly getting desperate.

"How much?"

Eli mentioned a sum that was three times what Robbie earned at the Double D for working with the horses. He was paid generously by Jack and to have figures in the thousands of dollars thrown at him was a shock.

"It's still a no."

If a man could pout, then Eli was doing so. He looked like a kicked puppy and Robbie narrowed his eyes when Eli unconsciously rubbed at his elbow. Had the idiot hurt himself when he fell? Sympathy welled inside him. The ground was hard from whatever height you fell.

"Can I just have a kiss then?" Eli said.

Sympathy for the guy disappeared in an instant. *What the fuck? A kiss? What the hell was this guy on?*

"No." And with that Robbie took the stairs to his room two at a time and shut the door behind him, locking it immediately. He didn't check to see if Eli had left. He wasn't fascinated by the guy with the intriguing green eyes and the ready smile, nor was he interested in the spikes of his dark hair, nor in the sense of living life that seeped from every pore of him. The guy was in-your-face adamant that he could get what he wanted and that was the last thing Robbie needed. If he was looking for someone to kiss, let alone fuck, he certainly would not be looking at Eli freaking Martin and his artistic view on the world.

Nope, despite what his dick was telling him, he wasn't interested at all.

CHAPTER 9

Eli just stood there for a few seconds. That was a first. Eli Martin didn't get turned down by guys he approached to model for him. Jeez, any pretty guy whom Eli offered work to was on him like white on rice. And if that session included kissing and maybe a bit of casual sex then who was he to turn it down? The guys were normally very grateful and he wasn't too shabby at showing them a good time.

Robbie was different from them; he wasn't some muscle-bound gym rat who posed and pouted, and knew the score. That *had* to be what intrigued Eli. He crossed to the house and waited for a few minutes before entering. He could hear voices inside but he wasn't ready for Riley's teasing. That was the oddest thing. He had people tell him he was so many things. A flirt with his models. An idiot in business and shallow with his relationships. He agreed with every one of them.

But something about Robbie intrigued him. When Robbie talked to Hayley he didn't treat her like a kid, he was polite, kind, interested in what Hayley was saying. He was comfortable in his own skin, a cowboy from the core of him to the battered hat he wore. Every line of muscle was natural, born of hard work and delineated by the sun. His skin stretched over a body that just begged to be caught on camera.

Eli was good at what he did; he captured parts of his models that others didn't. From their insecurities to their smoldering sexual intentions, his photos sold products.

Thing was, he had never begged a model, ever. Begging tall, blond, and gorgeous was a new one on him. It unsettled him.

"You coming in?" Riley asked.

Eli hadn't even noticed the door open. "He won't model for me," Eli said as he turned to face Riley.

Riley shrugged. "He's not a model. He's a cowboy."

Like that explained everything. Riley could sometimes be the master of understatement.

"I'll keep trying."

"Be careful with him, E. He's not like your other boys. There's a reason he ended up here and won't go back to Australia."

"What reason?"

"It's his story to tell." Riley's tone was patient and careful. Unspoken was the fact that other men could keep secrets as well as Eli with his illness.

Unease climbed inside Eli. Robbie didn't seem like a guy with too much he was hiding. And secrets? Well, Eli knew all about secrets.

Riley left then, moving back into the house, and after a few moments Eli followed.

Tomorrow was another day.

* * * * *

Robbie slumped down on his bed. No one since Paul had gotten under his skin like that freaking photographer friend of Riley's. Those green eyes of his, all sparkle and enthusiasm, with a gaze fixed firmly on Robbie, were unsettling. And what was all that shit about photographing him. Him? No way was he stripping and oiling and whatever the hell other cosmetic shit that models had to go through.

Fucking though… he could get with that program. He crossed to the mirror on the wall and looked at his face this way and that. There was nothing handsome about his face. In fact it all looked pretty ordinary to him. His blue eyes were clear, his lashes thick, but he wouldn't begin to describe his eyes as unusual or stunning or any of the other adjectives Eli had thrown at him.

"Like a sky just before a storm, all dark and brooding," Robbie parroted and then huffed his displeasure. His hair was thick and clean, if a little awry now the gel had literally fallen dead on the ground.

"Asshole," he muttered. "Yanking my chain."

Pulling off his T-shirt he folded it on the small dresser. Unbuckling his belt he caught sight of himself as he pushed his jeans down a little. His stomach was flat, he had what they called a six-pack, and his butt was more than okay. Although it took Paul some time to convince him about the butt part. And he had muscles.

"Can push you to the ground, Eli Martin," he said. It comforted him just to say the words out loud. There was no way to deny that a working cowboy had muscles. He wasn't particularly hairy—just a small furring of hair on his chest and around his nipples, and a little farther down. His dick was okay as well. A decent size as dicks went. But still. None of it added up to anything more than cowboy. Eli was playing with him, teasing him, and he didn't like it. He'd seen this kind of bullying before and it had ended up with his friend dead.

The knock on the door underscored Robbie's irritation. Pulling his jeans back up he moved to the door and flung it open with a snap.

"I said no—"

He stopped as soon as he realized who it was at the door. Not Eli at all, but Jack. Jack who had his hands up in a gesture of understanding—palms facing front and fingers spread.

"Riley sent me over," he began.

"He didn't need to." Robbie was trying to be respectful to his boss but his emotions and feelings were all over the place.

"He wanted me to say that you shouldn't pay Eli any attention."

"I wasn't," Robbie lied.

Jack forged on. "He said that Eli is going through this whole grabbing-life-where-he-can thing and that you are just in the way."

"Okay."

"He'll be gone by the middle of September."

"Gone?" Robbie said suspiciously. "What do you mean gone?" Gone in September implied not being gone now which implied he was staying at the ranch.

"He's staying in Momma's old room for the next few weeks."

Jack hesitated and Robbie watched the play of emotions across his boss's face. From resignation to pleasure, his frown turned to a grin right in front of Robbie's eyes.

"As long as he keeps his camera out of my face..." Robbie warned.

"I'll make sure to tell him," Jack said simply.

Robbie nodded and took the man at his word.

"Night, Robbie." He turned to leave and was two steps down when Robbie remembered what he wanted to say. He hesitated only for a moment; where his horses were concerned he could be very forceful.

"Jack, wait."

Jack stopped and turned.

"I'm thinking we need to call Neil in to look at the horses tomorrow. Just to get a veterinary check done."

Jack nodded. "I noticed Daisy isn't settling well. I'll organize it." Then he left. For a second Robbie concentrated on the horses, on the ranch, but all too soon his other concerns filtered through. Not least of which was that for some unknown godforsaken reason that hot sexy moron Eli was staying on the damn Double D.

Great.

Sleep was a long time coming and according to his watch he was awake every half-hour. In the end, with the dark of the night still black and impenetrable, Robbie pulled on jeans and made hot chocolate in his small kitchen. When not even that slowed him down he gave in to his gut feelings and left his loft. Taking the stairs two at a time, he landed with a thump at the bottom and then made his way right toward the entrance where the new horses were stabled.

The only noise in the stable beyond the normal snuffling and movement was the irritability from Daisy, and narrowing his eyes in the dark, he crossed to her stall.

She was nipping at her stomach and leaning against the wooden side. Shuffling from hoof to hoof, she was skittish and the sound she was making could only mean one thing. Climbing the gate, he landed lightly on his feet next to her and could see her heaving flanks for himself.

Hell, he'd never seen colic come on this fast. No wonder she was restless. And she was trying to roll to ease the pain. Fuck, that was always fatal if not addressed quickly. With not one second thought Robbie eased a halter over her head and clipped on a lead rope. After lifting the lock and pushing open the door with his hip, he led her out of her stall and walked her out into the cool night air.

"Okay girl, okay my Daisy," he crooned. He needed to call the vet or the house, but his freaking cell phone was in his room. Fuck. Next best thing… Jack.

He had no way to climb stairs to the front door, so Robbie led Daisy to the back where he knew Riley and Jack slept. Smacking the flat of his hand against the glass of the window he continued until finally the drapes pulled and Jack appeared at the window. Jack looked out at Robbie with Daisy, the drapes closed, and in seconds Jack was out by his side. In his hand he held a cell and was evidently making a call. Robbie listened as he walked Daisy in a large circle in front of the house. Her breathing was labored and for a second Robbie laid his cheek against her belly and whispered nothings to her. Even from here he could hear the noise curling inside her. Poor thing was probably in so much pain.

"Tell me," Jack ordered as he arrived.

"Went down to check. Couldn't sleep—"

"Me neither. Was just going to come check on her." Jack took the lead and urged Daisy to walk and between them they kept her walking until the lights of a vehicle broke the darkness.

"Colic I think," Robbie commented. Keeping her moving was important. If she went to the floor and rolled then her intestines would twist and it would be game over.

Two hours later Daisy was on a drip suspended from the rafters on a rope pulley. The needle was secured with duct tape so that she could move around.

"It shouldn't be more than a few hours until she starts to feel better," Neil said confidently. Jack yawned and Robbie glanced outside where daylight had forced the darkness out of the way. God knows what time it was. The three men slumped tiredly in front of the barn, their backs to the wood, and faces out to the new day.

"Thank you, Neil," Jack said.

"My pleasure," Neil answered.

"If it hadn't been for Robbie…" Jack started.

"You were up too… I just got there first," Robbie defended.

All three looked up when the front door to the house opened and Riley walked out followed by Eli. Eli with a freaking camera. Eli in designer jeans and a western shirt that was more style than substance. Before anyone could stop him the bastard had snapped a picture of the three of them sitting in a row exhausted and covered in God knows what.

Robbie was too tired to argue and he simply dropped his head between his hands, which were balanced on his bent knees.

"What's up with the photos?" Neil asked.

"That's Riley's friend Eli."

"Eli Martin." Eli introduced himself and held out a hand to Neil. Neil offered his left hand, which was covered in way fewer dubious deposits than his right. Eli crouched down in front of the three of them. "Tough night, eh?"

Robbie couldn't help the snort of laughter that he let loose. Suddenly sitting here exhausted and high from Daisy being okay, Eli in his faux-western clothes was the funniest thing on earth. The belly laugh was the first time he really remembered laughing properly since leaving Australia. Jack joined in and so did Neil until the three men were setting each other off as one stopped and another started.

All the time Eli was taking photos.

"I'm calling this a study in Cowboy," he announced.

Robbie sobered for a second. "You'd best run, Mr Photographer, or I'll steal the camera."

For some reason Neil and Jack found this amusing and the laughter continued.

"Coffee, Eli," Riley encouraged.

Robbie watched the two men leave. So different to look at. Where Riley was tall and lean and confident, Eli kept looking back at him, and really, he could stand to put on a little weight. Guy was far too skinny. Hot. Sexy. Gorgeous. But a strong wind and he'd fall over.

Hell. Maybe that was what happened the other night. Maybe the wind blew him over.

He just wished he could stop laughing at the image.

CHAPTER 10

The first models arrived two days after the incident with Daisy and two days after Eli caught Robbie on film. He should be concentrating on the photo shoot but all he could do was stare at the pictures of Robbie that sat on his laptop. In them his cowboy was sitting against the wood, his head thrown back in laughter or shyly lowering his gaze thinking Eli couldn't see him. He looked rumpled and hot and completely and utterly exhausted in every photo. And damn sexy.

Eli pulled himself away from the photos, to actually begin organizing the shoot. Spread over three days, it wasn't a simple 'point your camera and shoot'. There was lighting, makeup, and costume changes just so Eli could capture what the underwear company wanted. Of course, being an underwear shoot there weren't an awful lot of costume changes and there were one hell of a lot of flashed dicks and balls.

Normally Eli loved his job and for a few hours as he pushed and pulled and cajoled his team he was Elijah Martin, photographer. Then with one glimpse of Robbie standing to one side with unabashed curiosity he was suddenly Eli, horny man with a dick of steel.

Fuck.

What was Robbie doing staring at the half-naked models? Deliberately crossing past his team and ignoring all the calls of 'which', 'what', and 'why' he finally stood at Robbie's side.

"See something you like, cowboy?" he said with his best sexy drawl.

Robbie very deliberately looked past Eli to the group of chatting guys beyond. He shook his head.

"I don't do pretend," he said simply. And with that, and a grin, he wandered off back to his barn. A little later, while attempting to inject sexy into a bunch of prima donna models, he saw Robbie lead the horses one by one to the pasture. He didn't recall what Daisy looked like but assumed she wasn't well enough to—

"Eli?"

"Huh?" Eli pulled himself back to the here and now.

"The wood is chafing the models," his business partner Lauren advised. "And it's a bit hot."

Eli looked over at the pretty boys, all slim, some to the point of looking malnourished, and suddenly it all snapped.

"No."

"No?" Lauren looked confused. "Eli?"

"None of them are right. Where are my cowboys who are hot from working and with bodies and muscles... send them and all their chafing bits home."

"But Eli—"

"No. I'll call you." With this he grabbed two waters from the cooler and strode off in the last direction he had seen Robbie go. He left behind the models and the shoot and the come-hither glances from every single model there who thought fucking the photographer was their ticket to more. He didn't care. He was paid good money for the right thing. What he was shooting today was way past wrong. The guys who hired him would have to accept he knew best.

The sun was high and not for the first time today he wished he had worn a cap or something. He felt shaky, in fact he had felt off all day, a little nauseous and his head hurt. When he got back he really needed to take something for his headache and concentrate on drinking fluids. Otherwise he'd end up in the hospital. Again.

He found Robbie working with one of the new horses out in a far paddock, and he was hot and sweaty from the walk so far. There were three oaks that covered one corner a bit outside the field and Eli sought cover from the punishing midday sun. He watched Robbie; the play of his muscles, the movements so fluid and certain, the cowboy with his horse. There were moments of great affection; a touch on a flank, a gentle press of hands on a mane played against moments of strength and dominating will.

Jeez, I've never been this hard and so damn needy.

Leaving the water where he'd been sitting, he strode up to Robbie and the horse. Robbie turned just before he reached him. He looked surprised and then wary as Eli didn't stop walking until they were toe-to-toe. Whichever horse it was shook their head but didn't move as Eli did what he had wanted to do since the very minute he had met this roughhewn man.

He kissed him. Damn, he near climbed the guy. All hands and lips and want, and fuck if Robbie wasn't kissing him back just as hard and just as needy.

"Want you—" Eli demanded. Grabbing the back of Robbie's neck, he punished with the kisses. This was not slow and steady; this was desperate. Robbie finally pushed him back and Eli didn't argue. Both men stood there panting wildly, Robbie still with his hand looped through the guide rope holding the horse.

"What the fuck?" he stammered. He didn't shout, or scream, or rail, or accuse Eli of forcing him. If anything he sounded overwhelmed and uncertain.

"I want you," Eli repeated.

"You don't want me; you just want to fuck a cowboy—"

"Don't tell me I don't. Because I do. I want you. Only you. I want you inside me." Cupping Robbie's face and pleased when the other man didn't shy away, he kissed him gently. "You do things to me—"

"That's your dick talking," Robbie said crudely.

"No. Don't do that—"

"Do what? Tell the truth?"

"I'll give you back all the photos for a kiss," Eli said. He was aware there was desperation in his voice. "Every single photo I took of you when you didn't know—"

"Eli—"

"The ones where you are smiling and the smile reaches your incredible blue eyes. The ones where the weight of the world is in your expression and you look so damn sad. The ones where you are letting Jack in, and Riley, and when you joke with Hayley." Eli paused to let Robbie speak.

"You think you see an awful lot," Robbie finally said.

"I see that and so much more. And I want that more."

Robbie huffed irritably. "Sex—"

"I want more than sex." Eli grabbed at Robbie's hand. "Let's talk."

"Wait. Where are your models? Your work?"

"I'll explain later. Come on." Eli led Robbie and, by virtue of the fact Robbie held the guide rope, the horse as well until all of them were in the shade of the oak.

"Which horse is this?" Eli asked. They needed conversation of some point just to cool the hell down.

"Catty. She's a strong one. Gonna be a great barrel racer."

"Cool," Eli said, despite not really knowing what that meant.

"You have no idea what I just said, do you." Robbie laughed and Eli shook his head. "Do you want to know?"

"Please," Eli said. He settled himself down by the tree, sitting on the ground with his back against the trunk. He passed a bottle of the water to Robbie, who thanked him and then pointed up at Catty.

"She's going to be a good barrel racer because she has strong flanks and legs, and the musculature is typical quarter horse. Barrel racing is a rodeo event."

"Like with cows?" Eli didn't mean to sound thick but he didn't know and he really did want to understand. He had been to a rodeo before and he remembered calf roping and a clown. Other than that it was a blank of alcohol-infused fucking with the guy who took him.

"There's this clover leaf pattern that a horse and rider attempt to complete around preset barrels in the fastest time." Robbie hunkered down next to Eli and drew the shape in the dirt with his finger. "It is mostly a rodeo event for women and it combines the horse's athletic ability and the skills of a rider. It's fast and dangerous. Horses and riders can both get hurt. But the better trained the horse and the more disciplined and experienced the rider then the safer it is."

"I love listening to you," Eli said softly. He was feeling tired. Didn't matter he was cancer free. Sometimes exhaustion stole upon him with no regard for what he was doing or what he wanted to do. The docs said it was neurological shit; Eli tended to pay little attention to any of the negative stuff. He did what he was told and lived life by the day. Except… recently… seeing Riley and Jack together? Hell, anyone seeing the two of them together would want more. Way more.

"I can talk about horses forever," Robbie said. His admission held more than a little wryness and just a dash of being shy. The whole package was like this endearing invitation to sin.

Eli wanted more kissing but he felt a little lightheaded and admitted to himself that he was stupid to stalk out in the sun like he had.

"Sorry I jumped you." Eli was sorry really.

"It's okay. I kind of enjoyed it," Robbie admitted. He placed a finger over his lip. "Though I think I tasted blood." He half smiled. "Are you a wildcat in bed?"

"No!" Eli was horrified. Jeez. Robbie couldn't expect that long-term, there was no way Eli had the energy for all that climbing and jumping and mauling. Then he remembered the taste of this man and he somehow imagined he would love to be crawling and jumping all over him. "Sometimes, I guess."

"What?" Robbie asked seductively. He dropped to his knees from the crouch and took off his hat. Pouring half of his water over his head, he ran his hands through his hair as rivulets of water ran down his shirt. "You mostly a quiet one? All whispers and moans and slippery slow?"

Eli couldn't find his voice over the sound of his dick demanding instant gratification. Robbie leaned in the final distance and dropped the softest of kisses on Eli's lips, only deepening it enough to tangle tongues and taste each other. When they parted Eli had gone past turned on and was now a second from coming in his pants like a teenager.

"Want a hand with that?" Robbie asked. He reached down and flicked buttons open to delve inside until Eli felt the rough skin of Robbie's hand around him. "You're growing on me, city boy." Three movements, nothing more, and Eli was coming harder than he ever remembered from a hand job alone.

Then everything went dark.

* * * * *

"I told you. He was sitting against the tree and he just passed out." Robbie's voice. All concerned and gruff. "So I put him over the horse and bought him back."

"Should we get a doctor?" Jack asked.

"I don't know who his doctor is," Riley put his two cents worth in. "He may not even have one here. He was in LA for a long time."

No doctors. Please.

"Is his assistant woman still here?"

"No, they all left. We should get his cell."

"It's not in his pocket."

"Maybe we should phone the doc now. You don't just pass out like that—"

"It was hot," Robbie interrupted. "Maybe it's just dehydration."

"Robbie, he's not been well." Riley sounded so damn worried.

Eli didn't want to worry anyone. *I'm fine.* His tongue felt too big for his mouth and there was a gritty sandiness in his eyes as he forced them to open. *Still dark.*

"Is he still taking any medication?" Jack again.

"I don't know." Riley sounded pissed.

"I'll go." Robbie offered immediately.

"Idiot never told me he was gonna keel over. I assumed when he said remission that he meant he was well. Someone should check his room."

No!

"Wait. He's opening his eyes. Eli? Can you hear me? Eli? Eli?"

"Outamyfacefucker," Eli grumped at Riley. Damn man was hovering around him. Riley moved back.

"Do you need a doctor?" his friend asked.

"No. Water, sleep," Eli said. Between the three of them they managed to get Eli stripped to boxers and into his bed. Riley left and then Jack and finally as exhaustion pulled Eli under to a place where he could heal, he saw Robbie staring at him.

There was fear in the cowboy's eyes. Fear and shock. One single word had caused that. One word that haunted Eli every waking hour of his life.

Remission.

CHAPTER 11

Lauren was pacing and Riley even felt a little sorry for Eli. The man looked suitably chastised and was listening quietly to his assistant sounding off. Turns out she was less business partner and more close friend.

"They've given us an extension. But they said they'll be needing their deposit back if you don't come up with something. We can handle losing the money but your reputation, *our* reputation, will be for shit."

"Sorry—" Eli said.

Lauren interrupted. "Then you go and do some damn fool thing that leaves you unconscious in the dirt in the sun."

"He was in the shade," Riley offered helpfully. Lauren narrowed her gaze at him and Riley took a step back. That this itty-bitty woman who probably didn't top five-four was facing him down was a little bit of a culture shock. Reminded him of Donna actually.

"I was with someone," Eli defended himself.

"Dumb luck that you were. We organized this shoot so we could make everything easy for you—"

"Yeah," Eli said. "Too easy. All those models in their briefs draped over wood was like every single damn cliché in the book." He sounded grumpy but then Riley had experienced being laid up after he was in the fire and it sucked big time. He didn't begrudge Eli the small bit of angsting and whining that was seeing him through the day.

"What did the doctor say?" Lauren asked.

Eli threw his hands up in the air in a gesture of disbelief. "Now she asks. For your information I have a virus of some sort."

"Probably the same thing that had Hayley in bed last week," Riley said carefully.

"Yes. See? There's no cancer or anything."

Lauren's face crumpled. All the blustering and demanding dissolved in silent tears. Eli held out his hand. Riley watched with a lump in his throat as the two hugged and Eli was whispering he was okay, and Lauren was saying, "Don't go". They were like that for a while and finally Riley felt way too uncomfortable and went to find Jack. Anything for a break from yet more paperwork on the admin for the bids. He found his husband working with Daisy, who had perked up considerably. He loved watching Jack, the sinuous movements of horse and rider and the literal poetry in movement as Jack controlled Daisy.

"They're looking good out there."

Riley recognized Robbie's voice and turned to acknowledge him with a smile. He liked the guy. If they cut him in half he would have cowboy through the middle—just like Jack. Straightforward and down to earth, what you saw was what you got.

"Lauren's leaving in a bit if you want to go in and visit with Eli," Riley offered.

Robbie twisted his lips in a parody of a smile. "Not sure he'd want to see me."

"He asks after you every other word. Are you okay, what are you doing, are you freaked out?"

"I'm not freaked out."

"He seems to think you are."

Robbie was silent for a moment. "Cancer is a big thing."

"Remission is a big thing as well."

Robbie shrugged and focused back on Jack, who was working through the cool down.

"He's my friend, Robbie, and he's bored and worried and a million other things. Just for me, go and say hi?" Riley was unashamedly playing the husband-of-the-boss angle, and he added a smile as punctuation.

Robbie looked at him and then shook his head. Riley assumed the man was aware he was being manipulated but evidently wasn't going to call Riley on his bullshit.

"I will when I'm done seeing to Catty."

As he left, Jack walked Daisy over to Riley.

"You finished with paperwork?" He leaned over to kiss Riley and he tasted of fresh air and sweat and Jack.

"I was with Eli but his assistant turned up with the news he has to pull his finger out and come up with a new spread. Oh, and that she loves him." Jack raised his eyebrows. Riley laughed. "In a purely sister-brother type way. She said if he ever tries to die on her again she will kill him."

"Ouch," Jack said. He smirked. "Serves him right for whatever he was doing under the tree with Robbie."

"You think they were doing something?"

Jack stole another kiss.

"They say opposites attract. Hell, look at us."

"Meet you in the barn?"

"I need a shower, Riley."

Riley looked at his lover, sweaty and exhausted.

"Put your horse away, cowboy. Sweat or not, I want you in the barn in twenty."

Riley smirked as Jack pressed against his fly. "Jeez, Riley. Way to get me hard."

Riley turned on his heel and looked back over his shoulder as he walked away. "Twenty. I'll be waiting, spread naked over a stall door and ready to go."

As he passed the horse barn he looked in and saw Robbie rubbing down Catty. He was intensely focused on his task but clearly saw Riley out of the corner of his eye.

"Do you think you can help Jack with Daisy?" Riley asked.

"No worries." Robbie nodded.

Riley entered the cool interior of their barn and looked around. He felt peace here. This was where he fell in love, on this land, in this place, and here was home. Smiling, he opened their box. He had prep to do. Paperwork could wait.

* * * * *

Robbie stood silently at the door of Eli's room. Lauren had just left and although propped up in bed Eli had his eyes shut. Robbie bent his head briefly and considered whether he should announce he stood there in the doorway.

"You can come in," Eli said. "No sense in talking from the door."

Removing his hat and ruffling his hair, Robbie wondered if he should have stopped and had a shower first. He smelled like horse.

"How you doing?"

"I'm fine. I just sometimes do stupid shit that I shouldn't."

"How often?"

"What?"

"How often do you do stupid shit?"

Eli seemed confused by the question and then his face brightened. "Since the cancer? Twice. Once with champagne when I got the all clear. Expensive stuff, mind you. And once with you under the tree when you made me come in my jeans."

Robbie wondered briefly how to answer that one.

"Outside your jeans," he finally said. "Thank God. It was on my hands so I wiped it off and when we stripped you to your boxers no one knew."

"Thank you."

"For what? Bringing you back like a sack of potatoes on Catty's back? Or for making you come in your pants?"

"Both. Either." Eli shrugged. "So. Remission. You know about the cancer. Come and sit down so we can talk." He gestured to the chair by his bed but it was too close to Eli for comfort.

"I'm fine standing," Robbie said.

The way Eli's face changed, from hopeful to broken in an instant was one of the worst things Robbie had ever seen.

"It's not catching," Eli snapped.

Robbie stiffened. That was the first hint of temper he had ever heard from Eli. He didn't mean to make Eli angry. It's just that if he sat that close he would want to touch Eli and he wasn't sure the man would want that.

"I know that," he snapped back.

Eli shook his head at the response.

"You don't want to sit here near me then I tend to take these things personally. People don't want to sit with me, look at me, talk to me." He shrugged.

Robbie went with his gut feeling at these words and sat on the chair. He shuffled uncomfortably. What do you say to a man who was ill? Eli didn't give him a chance to say a single thing.

"I'm cancer free, you know. I'm in remission. I've been clear for a long time, nearly three years, so it's statistically unlikely that the cancer will return. Yes it was hard, no I don't think about it a lot, and no it doesn't affect my need to fuck or be fucked on a regular basis." There was that temper again. Sparking and hissing and spitting its way into the self-deprecation and sarcasm. "Now you can sit here and we can talk about where we go from here and what we want from each other or you can go so we don't start anything we can't finish."

"You can't dump all this on me and expect me to know all the answers. That isn't fair."

"Life isn't fair." Eli slumped back on his pillow. He looked better but still tired.

"You don't get it; hell, why would you, it's not like I've told you why I left Australia in the first place."

"I'm not going anywhere."

"I already lost one lover who died, and fuck, it nearly killed me. No point in starting anything only to have it end. Imagine what it would feel like to lose someone again." Robbie blurted the whole sentence out before he realized what exactly he had admitted.

Eli didn't call him on it. He just nodded. "So tell me about him," Eli said. His words weren't an order, more a plea.

"Paul? He was a cowboy, a buckaroo like me, and more than a good friend. Lots of lonely time on a station as big as we had, and we were both gay so we used some of that downtime and broke a little tension. Thing is, I fell in love and so did Paul, we even made plans for the future. Took this new guy, a big hulking brainless idiot, who decided fag was a word that suited Paul and me. I let it slide, Paul didn't. He always was a hotheaded guy. One lucky punch and Paul was on the floor. He never woke up. Had some kind of embolism that killed him fast inside. This was two years ago October and I tried to stick it out over there. Too many memories. I stayed for the trial when it finally happened. Then I left."

"I'm sorry."

"It's been a while now." Robbie wasn't entirely sure what else to say. That really was the whole sorry story, and enough to have him leaving the station and find his way home.

"Two years isn't long, you know," Eli stated simply.

"It's long enough. So, tell me your story."

Eli looked happy for Robbie to change the direction of conversation—he clearly didn't want to talk about Paul.

"I'd just been kicked out of college when I got sick. Just really tired and then I keeled over and had these blood tests, and it all kind of escalated from there. Kidney cancer. I was one of the lucky ones—I haven't lost an entire kidney and after treatment I was told everything looked good. Before cancer I was a bit lost, and a whole lot of a slacker. Plenty of ideas and opinions but no thought of acting on any of them. Except, of course, calling Riley Hayes a fucking asshole to his face and losing the only real friend I freaking had outside of my misfit excuse for a family."

"Riley?"

"That's a story for another day. The big C hits with a hammer and suddenly you are told if the next session of meds doesn't cure you then you have maybe six months to live. Amazing the shit you want to do when you only have six months left."

"Climbing mountains, spending all your money?" Robbie was attempting to lighten the tension but Eli simply shook his head.

"All I wanted to do was find someone who cared if I died."

That floored Robbie and he had no words to use. Instead something twisted in his chest. He *had* cared when Paul died. Cared enough to stay alive and leave. Was it possible there was room in his heart for someone else to care about?

Robbie hesitated momentarily then he forcibly relaxed every muscle until he sat comfortably on the hard wooden chair.

"So I guess we should talk more," he said. "You can tell me all about nearly dying and I can tell you about what it's like to be the one left behind."

"Then can we have sex?"

Robbie laughed loudly at the look of hope on Eli's face. "Maybe we could try dinner first until I'm sure you're not going to pass out on me every time you shoot in your pants," he said.

"Asshole."

CHAPTER 12

"What are you wearing?" Jack asked. He couldn't keep the horror out of his voice. Riley was distracted by checking e-mails on his cell and didn't immediately answer. "Seriously, Riley. What. The. Fuck?"

"What?" Riley looked up from the screen and blinked at Jack.

"Wearing?" Jack repeated.

Riley looked down at his jeans and boots and then back up at Jack.

"Jeans," Riley said. "You're wearing jeans. What's wrong with my jeans?"

Jack didn't know where to start. Riley's jeans probably cost a rodeo purse but yeah, he was wearing jeans. That wasn't the problem. Jack was indeed wearing jeans. Riley was also wearing a similar belt buckle to Jack. That is where all similarities ended. Jack was wearing a T-shirt and a western-style button-down in varying shades of blue and red. Riley was wearing a thin black T and a jacket.

That was the problem. The damn jacket was white, well, off-white, cream possibly. Hell, Jack didn't know, he wasn't a freaking clotheshorse like Riley was.

"You're wearing white to a rodeo."

Riley cast another look down and then slipped his cell in his pocket and realigned the jacket.

"It's a nice jacket," he defended. "It's Hugo Boss."

"It's white."

"It's off-white—"

"Riley. We're going to a rodeo—"

"A gay rodeo," Riley interrupted and emphasized the word 'gay' with air quotes. "You think the guys there are gonna turn up in range stuff with shit on their sleeves? I want to look good."

Jack held up his hands in defeat. "Have you actually ever been to a rodeo before, het-boy?" If Riley had, then he would know about the dust and dirt and the air ripe with curse words. A fashion show it wasn't.

"You know I haven't," Riley answered.

"Is it an expensive jacket?"

Riley didn't get a chance to answer as Hayley sashayed into the room holding Eden's hand and grinning. She was a miniature Jack, right up to a child's Stetson on her head, and Jack felt some satisfaction that their daughter had actually listened to him. Sean was a few steps behind Eden, and Jack could feel the focus shift immediately in Riley.

"Sean," Riley said carefully.

"Riley." Sean tipped his hat and then stood quietly.

Trouble was brewing between the two men—even a complete stranger could see that. It seemed to Jack that Riley had a point when he said Sean was messing with Eden. Still, Eden was in love and appeared happy.

"Momma's out front," Eden said. She was skilled at breaking up these Riley/Sean face-offs and all too soon they were all outside the ranch house and clambering into cars.

"You sure you're going to be okay?" Jack asked Robbie as he stood to wave everyone off.

"Eli's still sleepin' and I'll be working Daisy and Catty."

"If you wanted to go—"

"No. I don't."

Jack didn't argue. Robbie seemed happy on the Double D and very rarely left, even on his downtime. Still, he and Eli were spending a lot of time together, heads down and talking. Talking was good—it was way more than he and Riley had done when they first met. He guessed murders and fires and pregnancies kind of took the peace out of a new relationship.

"Jack?" Eden called.

With a nod to Robbie he took his seat in the brand-new 4x4 Riley had brought home a few weeks before. His Ferrari had long since gone and Jack didn't want to admit how much he missed that spitting, snarling dream of a car. When Riley nearly broke an axle coming down to the ranch in the dark it had to go. He seemed happy with the new car; top of the line, it did everything, except train the horses. Hell, it even spoke to you—all kinds of shit about the weather and business. Thankfully Riley had dulled the annoying voice to a gentle insistent background noise and instead seemed intent on increasing the discomfort between himself and Sean.

"So how was Afghanistan, Sean?" he said.

Jack sighed inwardly. Even for Riley that was a provocative question.

"Messy," Sean replied quietly. "A lot of good men dying on foreign soil."

"I imagine you've seen a lot," Riley continued. "Why do you need to keep going out there? Why don't you go back to writing books about horses?"

"Riley," Jack warned under his breath. Still his husband continued. Idiot needed a gag. And damn if the thought of that didn't make Jack hard. Jeez, it was like Riley was wired to his dick or something.

"I've seen too much. We all have there."

"So why go then?"

"I'm a journalist at heart, I go where the stories are," Sean replied. Such a simple answer but Riley had to be blind not to hear the tension in Sean's voice.

"Riley, how did it go with your bid?" Eden interrupted.

Thank God for little sisters who decided their big brothers needed cutting off at the source. Of course mentioning CH and its work was exactly the right thing to say. Riley could talk for hours on that subject.

Peace reigned for the journey after that. Especially when Hayley began chatting about her friend at school who had just got a new sister.

"I sometimes wish I could have a sister," Hayley said softly to Eden. Jack only heard because the reporter on the radio had just had a small moment of blissful silence.

"You would?" Eden asked.

Jack wanted to turn in his seat and look directly at his sister-in-law. He didn't. Instead he glanced at Riley who was concentrating on joining the freeway and apparently hadn't heard a thing.

"Sometimes." Hayley's voice was wistful and its effect twisted in his gut.

Jack looked out of his window and caught sight of his face in the wing mirror. He was turning thirty-two next March and the signs of working outside and his age were starting to show on his face. Thirty-two wasn't old but if he and Riley were to think about adding to their small family it probably needed to be soon. Didn't matter how much money Riley had—these things took time.

"You do realize, Ri, your jacket is going to last three minutes," Eden said.

Jack didn't think he had ever laughed as hard as he did when Riley simply huffed his response.

Jack had attended a lot of rodeos in his time; as a horse trainer and breeder it was his job to know people. He recognized quite a few big name stars and wished, not for the first time, that he had actually done his research on gay rodeo before he came out. He wasn't sure what he was expecting, it was a rodeo, it was loud and dirty and sweaty and testosterone to the limits, but it was different somehow. Guys walked holding hands with other guys, women hugged and kissed each other in front of Jack. There were drag queens and rodeo clowns, and Jack loved it all.

There were differences here. Whereas in mainstream rodeo there were traditional roles for men and others for women, in the gay rodeo every event was open to men and women alike. There were also extra events like dressing a goat, but luckily Jack wasn't involved in judging that—he wouldn't know where to start. Nope, he was there for the barrel racing and the finest display of horseflesh he had ever seen.

Riley was long since gone with Hayley in tow, and Eden and Sean had followed their noses and gone for barbecue, which left Jack leaning against the fence and watching the horses. He was due to judge the first rounds in a few minutes.

"Hey, Jack."

Jack turned at the voice and there was a face from the past. The distant past. Well, the past before Riley anyway. Austin Hemmings with the hoover suction mouth and the come-to-bed brown eyes. "What's it been? Five or six years?"

Jack moved back from the fence and shook Austin's hand.

"Has to be at least six."

"You're looking well."

"You are too."

"Heard you got married." And there was Austin, true to form, cutting straight to the point. "Where is the lucky man?"

"Off finding popcorn with our daughter."

"Hell, never took you as one to be domesticated, Campbell." Austin laughed.

Jack opened his mouth to correct his surname but suddenly what he really wanted to do was end this conversation and move on. Endings were never good but Jack had found Austin cheating on him and that was unacceptable. Not that Austin had thought anything was amiss. He was that kind of guy, strolling through his life with not much regard for others. Still a good-looking guy, he had the muscles of a cowboy and a look about him that spelled trouble. To this day Jack wasn't entirely sure what he'd seen in the other guy, especially now that he was with Riley. Riley was tall, Austin short, Riley was... hell, who was Jack kidding? The minute Riley walked into his life there was no man alive who could compare to his husband. Austin was leaning toward him saying something, words very definitely, but Jack wasn't listening. It was as if he had a Riley radar and when his husband's hard body pressed into him from behind Jack relaxed with an audible sigh.

"Riley Campbell-Hayes." Riley introduced himself and reached out around Jack to shake Austin's hand.

"Austin Hemmings."

Riley's hold on Jack momentarily tightened. There weren't any secrets between them now and Riley would remember what Jack had said about the only serious guy before him. "Pleased to meet you. Was just catching up with my man here."

"Uh huh." Riley was deceptively calm in his response.

Jack smirked inwardly. This show of possession was kind of hot. Austin clearly got the hint and took an awkward step back. All his swaggering bravado had dissipated in a few seconds.

"I need to go now. Nice to see you again." He tipped his hat and drawled, "Campbell."

"Campbell-Hayes," Riley corrected him.

Jack couldn't possibly love this man more than he did at that moment. Turning in Riley's hold as best he could, he reached up with both hands and drew Riley to him for a heated kiss. Right there. In the middle of the crowd waiting for the barrel racing. Right there in front of Austin. Catcalls and wolf whistles echoed around them, just another layer of sound in the noise around them.

"Hayley's gone with Eden for barbecue," Riley pulled back and spoke straight into Jack's ear. His voice was low and growly and all about possession. "You want some?"

Eat? Jack was having a hard time keeping himself from pushing Riley into a corner and kissing him till neither could breathe. Eating was not on his list.

"Mr Campbell-Hayes? We're starting now." The official who had come to find him was checking a clipboard with a smirk on his face and staring directly at Jack and Riley. Jack nodded. Now was his time to be a professional. Riley knew and he stepped back to lean against the fence where Jack had stood. Standing next to Riley, arms brushing, Jack didn't know how he made it through the first round of the racing with his dick hard and uncomfortable against his button fly. But somehow he did.

To see the quarter horses in the unique clover leaf pattern course, around the barrels, men and women alike, was to see poetry. Muscles bunching and releasing as the beautiful animals did what they did best. Jack watched and learned and realized this job wasn't going to be easy. Yes the winner was the one with the best time around the course, but he had the job of choosing best horse, best rider, best anything they could put on a list.

* * * * *

The restaurant was quiet and they were really the only people buying drinks at the small bar. Riley imagined it would be jumping in a few hours when the rodeo wound down, but for now it was kind of peaceful. Riley leaned against Jack and thought back over the day so far.

He'd never really had the jealousy thing before. Yes, Eli had mentioned how hot Jack was but that was nothing more than a throwaway comment. Seeing that ex, Austin, cozying up to his husband had made Riley want to come out swinging. Only holding and anchoring himself to Jack had kept him from leaping forward and smacking the guy to the floor. And wouldn't that look good in the papers? Not really.

He sighed.

"Who's pissed in your beer?" Jack asked with a smile.

Riley didn't even pretend not to understand what Jack was saying. His husband was on a high and here he was thinking on things long past. He checked that Hayley was still at the table—he didn't want her to hear what he had to say. He and Jack had promised honesty and that was what Jack was going to get.

"I could have hit Austin, you know."

Jack looked amused. "Only if you'd stopped me from getting there first."

"He was leaning into you."

"He was."

"I didn't like it."

"I didn't either."

"Oh." That was really all Riley could say to that one. Evidently Jack had felt the same way and probably hadn't needed him to interfere at all. "You probably didn't need me getting involved. Sorry."

"Hell, Riley. You draping yourself over me was hotter than a hot thing on a hot day." They nudged arms and Riley knew he had a great big sappy grin on his face. He was so far gone on this cowboy it was unreal.

"Just staking my claim, cowboy," he drawled in his best sleepy Texas accent.

Jack smiled and looked at him up then down. "Riley?" he asked. "Where's your jacket?"

"Under a bull," Eden interrupted as she gathered up Hayley's lemonade and hers and Sean's beers.

Jack let out a snort of laughter. "Under a bull?"

"It's a long story," Riley said with a wave of his hand like it wasn't important.

"Idiot here didn't want it getting covered in shit, was holding on to it and it got snagged on the gate. They opened the gate and there went the white—"

"Off-white—"

"—jacket. Under a bull and trampled into the dirt."

Eden and Jack were laughing big time now. Riley tried to act affronted, hell, he loved that jacket. He couldn't last long and soon he too was laughing with his sister and husband.

They made their way to the table in the corner and Sean immediately had his arm around Eden. Despite the laughter over the damn jacket Riley had just enough tension left in him that it transferred instantly to the man who was messing with his sister.

She wanted permanent, she wanted a husband and kids, and they may be engaged but Sean was not what she needed. He was a journalist, a good one, he had books under his belt, yet he still insisted on going off on these research trips. Why was he risking life and limb going to these crazy-ass places he didn't need to go? Putting himself in danger and making Eden worry was not what Riley wanted for his sister. Maybe he should make Sean some kind of offer, a financial incentive to stay in Texas.

Stupid idea. Eden would kill him. Hell, Jack would kill him.

"When do you leave for your next trip?" Jack asked.

"Day after tomorrow."

"How many more visits?"

Riley caught the end of a conversation and pulled himself together to listen. Sean was talking.

"Just this last one and I'm back in Texas full-time." Sean made it all sound so simple. Riley observed Eden gripping tightly to Sean's hand and could see the light dim a little in her eyes. She didn't want him going to wherever the hell it was and put his life in danger any more than Riley did.

"Then we're going to plan the wedding," she said.

"Can I be a flower girl?" Hayley piped up.

Thank God for small children breaking the tension. Riley looked on as his daughter and his sister discussed color choices and flowers. Sean listened with a smile on his face and slowly, very slowly Riley's irritability grew, which was stupid because clearly there was nothing he could do about it. He really needed to stow his big brother concerns. Eden wasn't a child and was plenty old enough to do all her worrying for herself.

"You okay?" Jack asked. He took a deep swallow of his beer after he asked and Riley pulled his gaze away from the way Jack was holding the bottle and the way his throat moved as he swallowed and instead focused on his husband's expression. Familiar blue eyes held concern and Riley kicked himself for being a downer on a day like today.

"I'm fine," he said. Raising his own bottle, he swallowed a mouthful of cold beer and decided to select a safe subject. "Why did you pick the red-colored over the white one for prettiest horse?"

Jack shook his head in mock horror and Riley smiled inwardly. He loved it when Jack got all horsey with him and he listened as Jack explained the differences between breeds and histories. Sean joined in with his own interpretation of the colors of horses and then Eden and when they were all laughing, Riley felt the tension leave him. Everything was going to be okay. Just because the Hayes family history was mired in tragedy and covered in shit didn't mean Eden couldn't be any less happy than Riley was at this very minute.

They left a little after nine and Riley carried their sleeping daughter from the car to the house. Jack unlocked the door and Riley took her straight to her room. There was no point in waking her up to get her to brush her teeth. Instead he simply removed her shoes and took off her jeans then covered her with the lightweight blanket. She mumbled something he couldn't understand and then reached up with sleepy arms. He came closer and went in for the patented Riley/Hayley snuggle. She smelled of the outside and of cotton candy and barbecue. He left her with a gentle kiss, pulled the door closed, and turned to find Jack there waiting. He stood with arms crossed over his broad chest and a look of expectation on his face.

"We need to talk," he said.

Riley felt his heart turn in his chest. Even after two years and knowing Jack loved him as much as he loved

Jack, those were words designed to carve fear into another person.

"What did I do?" Riley instantly said.

Jack looked confused and then gestured for them both to move away from Hayley's room and through to the kitchen. Riley noted through the open door as they passed Eli's room that the space was empty and that Eli wasn't asleep in bed.

"I meant about Austin."

"We don't need to talk about him." Riley couldn't have kept the relief from his voice if he'd tried.

"I just want you to know he came and talked to me. Not the other way around," Jack said so firmly that Riley immediately felt he should say something. Only he wasn't really sure what to say. He filled the coffeemaker and pressed the button to start the process. Jack always commented on Riley drinking coffee this late at night, said he wouldn't sleep, but Riley pointed out nothing except sex kept him awake these days.

"I know he did."

"I didn't ask him to touch me, or talk to me, or even freaking smile at me."

"I know." Riley repeated the words. "I didn't think otherwise."

"So we're good."

"Of course we are. Hell, didn't stop me getting jealous." He added the last with a smirk. Jack was pressing him back against the sink in seconds with his strong arms bracketing Riley and holding him in place. Riley shuffled his legs apart a little so they were equal in height and then he waited.

"You don't ever have to be jealous," Jack said.

"I remember you told me all about him. I know what he was like. It was the kind of stunt I would expect a guy who fucked around on you to pull." Riley reached up and carded his hands into Jack's hair. Gripping firmly, he guided Jack's lips to his and they settled into a kiss that was familiar and perfect. The slide of Jack's tongue and the taste of him, the feel of the smooth skin under the longer hair at the back of his husband's neck was so damned right. Riley could kiss and touch and just lose himself in Jack—the other half of him.

The knock on the door was gentle but enough to separate Jack from him and Riley cursed whoever was at the door.

"Sorry, boss," Robbie said. He had pushed open the door and looked a little embarrassed at having broken up the kiss.

"It's fine. Everything okay?"

"Daisy had a fine day. Catty is going through a stubborn stage, but we'll fix that soon enough. I had a message from Eli. He had to go into the city at three for this company that wants the photos. I didn't think you'd want him driving being as he's still unsteady on his feet, so I drove him in and I'm just going to pick him up."

"Do you want one of us to—"

"No. That's fine. I'm leaving now."

"Thank you, Robbie," Jack said simply.

Robbie nodded and pulled the door shut behind him as he left.

"There are some definite sparks there," Riley commented. He turned and watched from the window as

Robbie clambered into the ranch 4x4 and drove down the potholed drive. Jack pressed up against him, and Riley just enjoyed the feel of his husband hard and needy and strong behind him.

"Eli knows what he wants," Jack said.

Riley agreed. "Eli always knew his own mind and I think he has his mind set on Robbie."

"And Robbie's coming round to it."

"They're good together. The cowboy and the guy in a suit."

Jack pressed against Riley so that Riley was under no illusion how Jack was feeling at this moment.

"Sound familiar, het-boy?" Jack chuckled.

Riley turned in his hold as best he could. "Just a bit. Now take me to bed, cowboy, and show me who's boss."

Jack's eyes darkened at the words and he quickly drew Riley through the house without another word. Riley had heat building inside that he never grew tired of.

Not with Jack.

CHAPTER 13

Robbie pulled in to the drive of the large house he had dropped Eli at earlier that day. The edifice was still as imposing as it had been in daylight, even more so with the faintly sinister lighting washing upward from hidden lanterns in the undergrowth. He wasn't exactly good with architecture but the house looked very old and big and was probably incredibly expensive. On the drive here Eli had explained that the owner had made his money in men's underwear. Interesting way to earn a living and apparently a lucrative one.

Eli banging on his window pulled him out of his thoughts and he pressed the button to lower the window.

"Michael would like to meet you," Eli immediately said.

"I'm not exactly dressed for—"

"That's fine. Come on." Eli pulled the door open and Robbie was probably too shocked to argue. That was the only explanation he could think of when he looked back on what happened. He locked the 4x4 behind him and followed Eli up the six stairs that led to a huge porch area and an open door. A man stood there, older than Robbie, with gray hair, all dressed up in a suit and tie and with the widest grin. He was a good-looking guy, if you liked the silver fox type.

"Robbie," he said. "Eli has told us so much about you."

Robbie returned the smile and they shook hands. He had no sense from either man what was about to happen and he had no tools to draw on—he wasn't prepared.

"I told you," Eli said excitedly.

They were still on the porch and Robbie looked at Eli, confused. *Told him what?* He realized Eli was talking to Michael. The guy who was looking him up and down with an assessing leer and who actually laid hands on Robbie with a firm touch. Robbie didn't move. He was trapped between Eli and Michael and immobility was the result of a clash of shock and manners.

"And you can get ten or so others like him?" Michael was saying as he patted him.

Robbie was way past confused now but at least his muscles began to work independently of his brain.

"Easy," Eli said. "The gay rodeo is here in Dallas, I can go out tomorrow and see who'd be interested."

"This one has good bone structure. Interesting musculature. And I assume he's said yes?" Michael was talking to Eli but gesturing to Robbie.

What the hell? Are they talking about me?

"Of course." Eli's voice sounded odd and held a note of hesitation that he covered up really quickly. Robbie stared at him for clues as to what the hell was going on. "He said yes."

Eli's voice then took on that cocky tone that Robbie knew so well and finally the flag was raised and Robbie saw the whole picture. Before he could say a word Eli was pushing him down the steps and toward the car calling something back to Michael that Robbie couldn't even hear over the anger in his head.

"What the fuck?" Robbie snapped.

"Don't say anything out here, Rob," Eli pleaded.

They climbed into the car. Since when did Eli call him Rob? As soon as the door shut them in Robbie thought he would be safe to let loose with questions.

"What the hell was that about? What did you do, Eli?"

"I kinda promised I had proper cowboys and they said, Michael said, my contract would be extended so I can get the shots they need. I didn't think he was going to assume you were one of the models. I was just telling him how gorgeous you were and that you were all natural—"

"Eli—"

"What I said back there, when I said yes you had agreed, I just needed to get him off my back. I'll just tell him your test shots were crap."

"He looked at me like..." Robbie was flustered and furious. He couldn't find words enough to cover the horror of being checked out like a prize bull. Fuck, he could feel Michael's gaze still all over him and the firm touch of his probing hands pushing at muscle and testing bone.

"I'm sorry. That is what he does." Eli was apologizing—Robbie could hear the words but they were empty platitudes. "He could make or break my business."

"Let me get this straight. You took me in that house so that your creepy client could check me out as a freaking nude model for a photo shoot he wants me in that isn't going to happen over my dead body?"

"Not nude—"

"Semantics, Eli."

Eli slumped a little and leaned on the door. His body language radiated defeat as if he was giving up on the discussion. Robbie immediately jumped to conclusions.

"That's it?"

"What's it?"

Was Eli being deliberately stupid here?

"You're client eye raped me, touched me like I was cattle, and you're fucking sulking now?"

"No." Eli straightened in his seat. "I don't sulk."

Useful that he didn't address the other things Robbie picked up on. Robbie started the engine and pulled out of the circular drive.

"Sure looks like it," he snapped. "Put your belt on."

Satisfied when Eli did as he was told, Robbie joined the flow of traffic. Robbie was seething but the fifty minutes or so it would take from here to the Double D would be bearable if Eli just sat back and shut the hell up. Never let it be said Eli could sit quietly for any more than a damn minute.

"He just wanted to meet you," Eli said. "He wanted to see what kind of man I had in mind. I didn't know he was going to treat you like..." Eli's voice trailed away.

Robbie wasn't going to attempt this conversation, not when anger skimmed and hissed just under his skin.

"I don't want to talk about this anymore," he said. Robbie felt all kinds of things: angry, insulted, and ultimately embarrassed that Eli would put him in that position.

"Look, I fucked up. I'm sorry."

"Whatever." Robbie cut that particular line of bullshit dead and concentrated on driving back to the place he called home.

"Now who's sulking," Eli said wryly.

Was Eli joking? If that short sharp comment was meant to break the uneasy silence then it wasn't going to work.

Robbie refused to answer and the rest of the journey was spent in an uneasy silence.

When the 4x4 stopped outside the ranch, Robbie had the engine off and was out of his door before Eli had managed to undo his belt. In seconds he was at the steps to his room and as soon as he heard Eli shut the door of the car Robbie locked the vehicle remotely. There was no way Eli would catch up to him, and when his apartment door was shut to the outside Robbie let fly a torrent of curse words at the stupidity of it all. There was him thinking Eli was a good guy when in fact all he had been was one huge fucking asshole. Business or no business, he'd thought Eli was becoming a friend with a view to more. He evidently knew that Michael guy, being as he was Eli's client, and probably knew exactly how Robbie would be treated.

Half of him hoped Eli would come to the door just so he could deck the guy, remission and virus or not. Eli didn't. When Robbie checked out of his small window he could see Eli letting himself in the main ranch and the light going on in the kitchen. Pushing himself up and away from the frame he stalked to his bed, pulled off his clothes in an economy of motion, and went to bed.

Okay, so he didn't sleep, but it was a hot sultry night and he blamed the heat.

The warmth of his temper and his embarrassment didn't help.

* * * * *

Eli attempted to be quiet but it had never been his strong point. The house was in darkness apart from the kitchen and he assumed Riley and Jack had gone to bed for the night. He had a beer and a bag of chips in front of him on the table when Riley walked in.

"Go okay?" Riley asked as he yawned.

"They're happy with the new idea," Eli said. There was caution in his voice and if he could hear it then so could Riley.

"What's wrong then?"

"Nothing." *Lying is easy.*

Riley sat down next to Eli. That in itself was odd. If Riley wanted to sit down wouldn't he be better off opposite Eli? This could only mean one thing. A chat.

"Are you feeling okay?" Riley asked.

Sudden irritation built inside Eli and he grimaced. Just because Riley knew about the cancer didn't mean he had to ask Eli all the time if he was okay.

"Fine," he snapped.

Riley turned in his seat and his hazel eyes were filled with empathy. Gently he placed a hand on the one Eli had resting on his chest. Shit, he hadn't even realized it was there.

"Then why are you sitting here looking so miserable and pressing your chest like your heart hurts?"

"I fucked up."

"You need to talk?"

Eli considered the offer for a while. How did he admit to Riley he had been an idiot who had hurt Robbie, and that he didn't even really need to discuss that fact, he just needed to know how to apologize. The whole sorry story slipped out in rapid sentences.

"I want to use real cowboys for the photo shoot and Michael said this was a brilliant idea but he didn't understand what a 'real' cowboy could look like. So when Robbie picked me up—and God, Robbie is hot, right?—I asked Robbie in and Michael assumed he was a model and was all over him like a rash. Robbie is pissed at me because I didn't correct Michael." Eli paused for breath. "See, you have a cowboy, right?"

Riley's gaze widened and his mouth fell open in a perfect O of surprise.

"You are not using Jack in your shoot." His words were almost as fast as Eli's explanation.

"I wasn't. I wouldn't. You're not listening to me. I hadn't finished."

"Go on then. This is going to be a good one." Riley sat back and away from Eli and waited.

"How would you apologize to Jack and not make it come over as pathetic? I should have realized what Michael would do and even if I hadn't I should have just said that Robbie was my..." His voice trailed away. What was Robbie to him exactly? Friend? Potential lover? The guy he wanted to climb all over and kiss from head to toe?

"Yes, you should." Riley started evenly. "But jeez, if you heard about some of the idiotic things I did and said to Jack you would wonder why he stayed with me. Nothing's perfect. Leave Robbie to calm down. If he's anything like Jack, all calm on the surface but heat underneath, then his temper will be hot. You let him get his reaction out of the way, and then you can use the patented Eli charm to make him see you are not a complete loser."

The two men sat in silence for a while.

"Do you remember that time you rappelled from the dorm roof using the telephone cable?" Eli asked. He wanted to settle the terror inside him that he had fucked up this whole Robbie thing big time. College memories, before Lexie/Riley and before he crashed the damn car in the lake, were safe ones.

Riley didn't look surprised by the change in direction. They had exchanged a few stories like this one since Eli had gotten back in touch. Riley flexed his hand and winced.

"I remember the sprained wrist," he answered. "And the look on Booker's face when I landed on him."

"I laughed so hard I nearly peed myself." Eli laughed.

"I think Booker actually peed himself."

"Ri?"

"Uh huh?"

"You're happy with Jack, aren't you? I mean, it's obvious how happy you are. I wasn't really meaning that as a question. When did you know you were in love with him?"

"Really? You mean the actual time I felt like there was something more than irritability and sex between us?" Eli nodded at the question. "I don't know. Not really. I was heartless to start off. I remember feeling like I had pulled off the greatest business transaction of my life and feeling proud of myself when I convinced him to marry me. Then suddenly I wasn't so proud. Maybe it was the horses. Or the Double D. Or his sister Beth. Sometimes I wish I could pinpoint the absolute time."

"The time matters to you?" Eli asked.

"No, not really. All that matters is that every time I see him now I fall in love with him all over again."

"What if I told you something that is going to sound real crazy."

"You mean like every other time you open your mouth?" Riley smiled.

"It's been such a short time but I want Robbie. No, I want more than that. I need Robbie. If having cancer has taught me one thing it's that you don't fuck around with the life you have."

"And how does Robbie feel? Have you told him this?" Riley reached again to still the hand that was pressed to Eli's chest, stopping it from moving.

"Before or after I reduced the potential of anything at all to a heaping pile of horse shit? No."

"So you tell him. In the morning. Now, it's past midnight and you get to bed, get some sleep, and stop worrying."

"Yes, Mom." Eli smirked.

"Ass." Riley released his touch and left the kitchen with a waved 'later'.

Eli sat for a while. Nursing his warm beer with no real intention of drinking it, he looked up and out of the window and over to the barn. Robbie was in there, probably pissed as hell and feeling like Eli had treated him like shit. He stood and even took a step toward the door. Some nebulous thought in his head was telling him to go over now and sort this out. Thing is, there was really nothing to sort out. Eli was a loser and Robbie had seen his true colors. Kind of inevitable really.

Why the hell hadn't he thought about what was happening? It wasn't like he needed the money from Michael and he could say what he damned well wanted to the man who needed his photos. Suddenly his skin felt too tight and scratchy, and irritated with himself, he made sure the door was locked and then turned off the light.

Bed sounded good. He just hoped he could sleep.

When he woke he knew Riley would have left for the office, Hayley would be at school, and Jack and Robbie were likely in a far field working the horses.

He'd never felt so lonely.

CHAPTER 14

With Hayley at a friend's birthday it was only Riley who accompanied Jack to the second and final day of Jack's part of the Rodeo. Today was prize-giving day and proved to be more hectic than even the hours they had spent there before. Riley was proud of the man who so confidently appraised horses and riders. Other men regarded his husband with a combination of awe and some very definite lust. Who wouldn't look at Jack with lust; it was something Riley did every damn day. He amused himself with a combination of watching Jack and the other cowboys and cowgirls who streamed from one event to the other. The barrel racing may well be the part of the rodeo Jack was judging, but to be honest Riley was drawn to the bull riding.

It was something about the power in the rider's arms and legs, the strength of muscles that tensed and released with the violent movements of the bull they were riding. The clowns were bright and welcome when a participant hit dirt and the bulls were big and nasty and dangerous. A couple of times Riley noticed Austin Hemmings in the periphery and wondered if the guy was here to compete. The irrationally jealous part of Riley wanted Austin to last no more than two seconds on the bull's back before landing on his ass in the dirt. Safely of course. No broken bones or goring. Riley wasn't entirely evil in his thoughts.

Austin was with another cowboy, a tall skinny guy with spiky blond hair, a skin problem, and an attitude. The hair and skin Riley had seen when the other guy knocked into him, up close and personal, in the line for burgers. The attitude was obvious from tall-and-skinny staring right at Riley with a sneer of contempt. There was something in those eyes that threatened violence and the scent of beer on the guy's breath hit Riley like a brick. Riley hoped to God the man wasn't bull riding or going anywhere near any livestock in this rodeo; he looked frustrated and angry and just plain drunk.

"See you met my friend, Hayes."

Riley deliberately looked at the retreating skinny guy and then back to the one person he was trying to avoid. Austin *freaking* Hemmings.

"Friend?" Riley said. He immediately regretted saying anything as Austin's eyes lit up with an unholy glee.

"Another one of Jack's exes," Austin said. "Surprised Jack didn't make you a list."

Riley shrugged. He wanted to say something quick and witty and profound. Hell, what he really wanted to do was pound Austin into the dirt.

"Not bothered about the past," he said. That was his way of cutting Austin dead. He tipped his hat and walked away without looking back, although he could feel the weight of Austin's stare. Quite apart from circling Jack and pissing in a circle around him there was only one way he could think of reinforcing his claim on his husband. Failing full-blown public sex he settled for eating his burger and then finding Jack for a kiss or a hug or something.

Finding Jack was easy. He was sitting on a gate—at the center of a group of similarly dressed guys and two girls, all chatting away about horses and training, and Jack's expression was animated. Riley could watch the man all day but really, he should make himself known.

"Hey, cowboy," Riley said.

"Riley!" Jack's eyes lit up. "Guys, this is Riley." Jack slid off of the gate and pulled Riley to him in an embrace. Riley leaned into the hug and grinned at his husband. There were more catcalls and a couple of suggestive remarks before Riley moved to one side. Standing here together, with his fingers threaded possessively through Jack's belt loops, Riley had never felt happier. Austin walked past and glanced briefly at Jack. There was a frown between Jack's eyes but it cleared when someone spoke to him.

Something about Austin Hemmings made Riley's gut turn.

* * * * *

"You want to get out of here?" Jack had finished his part of today's festivities and the rodeo was quieting down for today.

"You sure? You all done?" Riley didn't want Jack to have to leave early on his account. He was enjoying seeing his husband being the center of attention and dealing with it so well. He couldn't have been prouder of the man he married.

"I need a beer, a shower, and you. In that order."

Riley smiled. He could get with that. "Rusty Nail?"

"Rusty Nail."

Despite the brawl they'd taken part in a few years before, the Rusty Nail welcomed Riley and Jack on a frequent basis. The bar in the middle of nowhere was a rundown place that only remained standing, in Riley's opinion, due to dirt and willpower. The beer was cold and the food was hot, it was close to the Rodeo and that was exactly what he needed.

The bar itself was halfway between the showground and the Double D, and they made it there in good time. Jack was quiet and had slid down in his seat a little on the journey over but he was bright-eyed and bushy-tailed as soon as they arrived.

Steaks ordered and beer in hand, the two men ensconced themselves in a corner and people-watched. A lot of the rodeo participants had made their way here. The bar was a good place to shoot the breeze and not feel like you had to be something different than you were. The air was ripe with laughter and cursing and congratulations to winners. Riley relaxed inch by inch, and to his credit only tensed a little when Austin and skinny guy walked in with two or three other cowboys.

Riley debated telling Jack what Austin had said about the list. But knowing Jack's temper it would probably not go down so well. Instead, he pointedly ignored even thinking about the guy and turned his attention to Jack, who was talking to him.

"…noticed he was a little spaced out."

"Sorry?" Riley had clearly missed something.

"Sean." Jack tilted his beer and swallowed a good amount in one go. "Said I thought when I saw him yesterday he looked kinda spaced out."

"I noticed that." Riley bristled at the memory. The guy was all over Eden like a rash, and yeah, Riley liked the guy, but something was going on with him. If Jack had noticed too then maybe he should get a PI to tail Sean and see what was going on. He'd better not be cheating on Eden or—

"Riley!" Jack was snapping fingers in front of his face and Riley startled. "Wherever you freaky brain is taking this you need to take a step back. He clearly adores Eden, I just think maybe, on his last trip overseas with the Marines, he could have experienced some things that make a man stop and think."

"So why go back?" Riley leaned back in his chair and huffed his disapproval. "He doesn't need to do that. He's not a forces guy, he's a goddamned civilian."

"Would you respect him if he stayed here and didn't finish out his contract? Do you want that kind of guy for your sister?"

Damn Jack and his ability to cut through the bullshit.

"She's my sister," Riley said helplessly.

"Let him know how you feel. At least then you can stop worrying that he doesn't know how it affects you. Talk to him, het-boy."

Riley smiled at the familiar nickname, and their conversation was interrupted by the arrival of their food and another beer for Jack. Riley was driving and one beer was enough now that he was a responsible daddy and husband.

They ate companionably for a while. The noise of the growing crowd made intimate conversation difficult anyway and when they had finished, they both stood to leave by silent agreement.

"Going so soon, Jackson? Husband got you whipped?"

Austin's voice was loud, raucously so, and right in Riley's ear, causing him to jerk away in surprise.

"Little jumpy, aren't we?" Austin added with a laugh.

Riley looked to Jack but his husband was pointedly ignoring Austin and shrugging on his jacket, ready to leave. Riley took a step farther away from Austin.

"Fuck off, Austin," he snapped.

Jack nodded and together they made their way through the crowd toward the door. Jack was swallowed by the crowd and Riley got snagged up by two cowgirls who evidently thought he was a stripper's pole. Laughing, he encouraged them to one side and then continued to catch up his husband.

Someone grabbed at Riley's jacket and caught him off balance—able to haul him close. Austin. The guy's breath smelled of hard liquor and beer and Riley grimaced.

"Bet he spends more time fucking with his horses than he does fucking you," Austin said. "You like cowboys? You get tossed by him like I was and you're horny, come find me."

"I said, fuck off." Riley pulled his sleeve free but it appeared Austin wasn't finished.

"He was a shit fuck anyway—"

Riley lost it between one heartbeat and the next. Worry about Sean and Eden had started the irritation inside him and the crowd pressing in around him and now Austin giving attitude and shit just made it worse. Anger rolled through him in a wave and he spun on his heel and hit fist to flesh in a second. The sheer number of people stopped Austin falling to the floor but quite a few drinks spilled, and the mood of the crowd went from mellow to what-the-fuck in seconds. Austin was pushed back, and with the weight of his body behind him, he aimed straight at Riley's face. Riley managed to dodge the blow enough so that the hit connected with his neck but regretted the move as soon as dizziness forced him to grab hold of the nearest body to stay upright. That same body pushed him away and this time Austin's fist connected with Riley's chin.

Riley saw red. He blocked the next hit and then, using his superior height, he followed through with several punches. Skinny guy was there at his left and Riley tensed as he now had two assailants in this crowd. A hand yanked at his arm and dragged him backward.

"We're moving this outside." Jack's voice.

Riley tried to pull back but as he stumbled out into the fresh air he realized Austin and skinny guy were following as was a group of hangers-on who evidently wanted to watch.

"What happened, Riley?" Jack asked urgently.

"I hit him. He hit me," Riley answered and took a step toward Austin. Austin took a step back and Riley could see he was nursing a broken nose. Chalk that up as one for the office guy.

"He's an asshole," Jack said firmly. "We're leaving."

"That's right—take your pretty boy home before I stomp him in the dirt, Jacky boy," Austin threatened from the safety of the group of people around him.

Silence.

"What did he do, Austin? Hmmm? Did he dismiss you out of hand? Did he call you on your bullshit?" Jack was deceptively calm. Riley could see the temper in Jack's eyes and feel the ice that dripped in his voice. "He's a bit big to force yourself on though…"

Gradually as Jack spoke, one by one, the small group of watchers melted away until only the four men remained.

"Now Jack—"

"Austin, you're going to want to turn around and take yourself back into the bar," Riley said. He deliberately stood between Jack and Austin. "Else I think Jack'll hurt you."

The men stood in a face-off until with a loud "fuck" Austin turned and walked straight back into the Rusty Nail, skinny guy following.

Riley couldn't stop the huff of a laugh that left his mouth and when he turned to Jack he saw a familiar smile on his husband's face.

"You enjoyed that," Jack said.

"He deserved it," Riley replied.

"Wanna go home now, het-boy?"

Riley gripped Jack's hand and together they walked to the 4x4. They stopped at Jack's door. Gently Jack cradled Riley's face.

"You're bleeding," he said. He wiped at blood on the corner of Riley's mouth and then, with a soft press of his lips, he sealed the hurt with a kiss.

Riley melted. Right there in the parking lot of the Rusty Nail with someone's jealousy and anger marked into his face he fell in love with Jack all over again.

CHAPTER 15

When Ernst Christian turned up at his office without an appointment Riley knew something was wrong. This assumption was backed up by the way Ernst shut the door behind him. Not only that, but there was a very serious expression on his co-investor's face as Ernst carefully placed the sheaf of papers on Riley's desk. Ernst was another stalwart in the Texas oil industry and had never really seen eye to eye with Gerald Hayes, one of the reasons Riley approached him to be part of the first CH consulting project. When he agreed to place money behind Riley's first foray into ethical exploration he had shaken his hand and said he had faith in Riley.

Riley remembered those words to this day.

He glanced down at the paperwork and recognized the CH logo. The papers were the bound copies of the research report backing up the potential ten percent increase on returns and the investment in local economies.

"Would you like coffee?"

"No."

"Something stronger?" Riley was asking out of politeness but Ernst waved it away. Evidently this was more important than the usual business hellos.

"Someone gave these papers to me today. I think you should look at them."

"The reports from CH?" Riley said. "The ones from the meeting?"

"The person who gave them to me claims that the calculations and assumptions you used were based on falsified results and that these new copies are of the originals you amended."

"Who gave them to you, Ernst?"

"Is it true?" Ernst looked pale. As well he would. Inaccurate figures at this stage could get them the contract with the inability to fund the work, which would incur huge fines and then cut severely into any small perceived profit. Riley was well aware Christex Oil was in some financial trouble. He tried not to take it personally.

"You are asking me if the paperwork I supplied you with to inform your decision on this investment was falsified in any way?" Riley refused to feel accused. "Then I say no. Whatever you received from me is the correct data. This version of the report is nothing more than lies."

"My analysts looked at it and they say what is in the new report, which looks to be from your office, makes for some very interesting reading. They say the differences are subtle enough so as not to make much difference to an untrained eye. But they can't be sure one way or another which is correct without going back to the very beginning of it all."

Riley held his frustration very close to him. They were literally days away from hearing if their bid had been accepted. Financially he probably could stand to lose one investor but to lose Ernst and maybe some of the others who had been fed the lies in an altered report? That would leave CH unable to take this bid forward. They were so close.

"Who gave you this new information and implied I had withheld something from the syndicate?"

"Josiah Harrold."

Riley sat back in his chair. What possible benefit could Josiah gain from stopping a deal at this late stage? He was as exposed as the next man in this small team of investors. He stood to make a huge profit despite only getting twenty percent when he had demanded thirty.

Ernst continued. What he said made everything absolutely clear.

"He's been working up an alternative consortium—says he already has four investors and wants us to move over to what he says. Our percentage would be lower, it's not an equal split, but he says he has an alternative in place. Going in at a much more reasonable level of bid, cutting back on some of the ethical concerns, maybe hiring outside of the county..." Ernst's voice trailed away. He looked confused.

If there was one person in the group Riley thought would have his back it was Ernst. He was a good man under incredible pressure in both his private life and financially since the Gulf spill. Riley respected him.

"The point of CH consulting is to assist companies like yours to create local jobs and to be a positive force in the economy while balancing the needs for fuel—"

"Josiah said we can't rely on your —"

"This was the reason why you came on board, Ernst. You said you wanted more for your inheritance than some old seventies oil company with no thought for anything past money."

"That isn't the point, Riley. I'm nervous. I want to believe you wouldn't screw us over, but, hell, I don't know you as well as I should, son. Is what Josiah said true?"

"I said no."

"You know how much money Christex has tied up in compensation schemes."

Ernst looked tired and Riley went to the mini-fridge in the corner of his room and pulled out two beers. He cracked the tops and handed one to Ernst, who took it without hesitation. Swallowing half the bottle's contents in one go he then straightened in his chair. "You have to know that I'm considering withdrawing from the syndicate."

"Ernst, you've spent so long working with me to get to this stage. I can take your analysts through the entire setup to approve the figures again. Reassure you that what I am doing here is sound."

"It isn't that, Riley. You have to know that Josiah has put in a rival bid and has asked myself and the others to push our investment his way."

"Using my research," Riley said. He couldn't help the bitterness in his voice and felt the need for revenge well up inside him. Clearly the feelings inside were showing on his face as Ernst held up a hand in a gesture of defense. Riley forced himself to calm down. He wasn't angry with Ernst, it was a different target he had in his head.

"I'm not saying yes to him. But what if Helmes and Masters do? You and I couldn't pull this off on our own and I can't risk the financial exposure."

Riley considered what Ernst was saying. He was right. What if Helmes and Masters jumped ship to Josiah and then Ernst did the same. That left Riley with an unworkable bid and months of work wasted.

Holding up a hand he simply said, "Wait."

First call—his dad. Second one to Jack telling him he would be home late. Then calls to both Helmes and Masters asking them to meet. If Josiah was trying to screw with him then he had chosen the wrong man to do it to. Should they meet here? Maybe his office was too obvious? Josiah would expect Riley to call a meeting if anyone leaked details of this new consortium. They needed somewhere better to meet away from prying eyes. Hayes Oil had security and suddenly Riley sensed whatever happened next had to happen in the Tower. A theatrical backdrop to a dramatic impasse.

* * * * *

Riley hadn't been inside Hayes Oil for a long time— maybe three or four months. The smooth ride in the elevator to the sixty-fourth floor was as quick as he remembered and little had changed since the days he'd worked in the map room and Gerald and Jeff Hayes played with the oil world like it was their own personal toy. Hayes Oil was different now. Slowly but surely the management team in his family's place was turning things around and for a second Riley stood and inhaled the scent of carpet and fresh paint. He was proud of what was happening here, proud of any legacy he was leaving for Hayley and her children. Then there was Jack—this is where it all started sixty-four floors above the city when he first really met Jack.

"Sir." A girl he didn't recognize approached him. "Your guests are in the conference room and everything you asked for has been made available."

"Thank you."

"I'll bring in the coffee in a few minutes, sir."

"Please call me Riley. Thank you. Is my father here yet?"

"No, but he left a message for you—to say he has stopped off for something important." She read this from a note in her hand. Riley wondered what that meant, but only briefly as she began to lead them to the conference room.

Ernst followed him into the large room and for a while the men inside—Ernst, Helmes, and Masters—exchanged pleasantries like the whole of the CH proposal wasn't being flushed down the toilet.

"I assume you received the same paperwork and informal chat from Josiah?" Riley directed his question toward Helmes and Masters. Oscar Helmes simply sniffed and waved the whole thing away.

"Bullshit," he dismissed. "Josiah has some kind of bee in his bonnet about working with CH and he's left it this late to jump ship so your proposal would be dead in the water. I didn't believe a word he was peddling."

Bill Masters was a little less exuberant in his dismissal of what Josiah had been proposing but he did sum up the situation quite nicely.

"Didn't worry me," he said.

"None of you are as exposed to the market as I am," Ernst said. "I've put an awful lot of faith in young Riley's company but if our offer is accepted and I don't see returns in the first twelve months then you may as well kiss goodbye to Christex."

Riley observed as Bill and Oscar looked at each other. The three men, Ernst included, were what was left of the old oil. Add to that Josiah, and Riley was pretty much facing the only people of Gerald's generation left. Doubt filtered through him. Why did he choose these four men to get into bed with? Was it trying to kick Gerald's teeth? A final 'fuck you' to the man who he had called dad for so long?

"I'm assuming, Riley, that we are sitting here as a new syndicate without Josiah's input," Oscar said.

Riley nodded. "I'm not forcing any of you to take the stance of playing on the CH team as opposed to going with Josiah." He didn't need to say the obvious—that Josiah had deliberately sabotaged the small syndicate and at the last moment so that there would be no way of CH recovering this ground. "The choice is yours. The original deal, based on my company's accurate and audited research, is here in this room with Josiah's name on it as a partner next to all of yours. Clearly he has an issue with that deal, and has commissioned his own studies to form a new group of which I assume you three are part of."

"He said you had changed the figures." Ernst was clinging to this worry desperately. "Said his version was some kind of original he had uncovered."

"Every step of this process has been transparent," Oscar interrupted. "My money is with Riley and his consultancy backed up by the information my own analysts assessed. I saw the work Riley used to do for Hayes Oil, and even though he was never given credit, I trust his oilman's instincts."

One down. Two to go. There was a silence and Riley waited for who was to speak next.

"Agreed. I'm sitting this one with Riley also." Bill sat back in his chair and visibly relaxed as he made the decision.

That left Ernst who had his hands clenched in his lap and was visibly tense.

"I'm thinking of pulling out all together. No CH, no Josiah."

"That's your choice, and none of us here will stop you from making your own decision," Riley said. In his head he began calculating what they would need to finance the gap of losing two syndicate members. His stomach sank when he realized just how much he would need to find to fill the hole. He could have managed one loss of the five, but two? He wasn't even sure changes to the syndicate at this late stage would be something the government agency would fly with, whatever kind of group they were left with after today. Fucking Josiah and his crippling move of sowing seeds of doubt.

The door opened and his dad arrived with his mom in tow. She was dressed as Riley remembered from the time before she broke free from Gerald and found love again with Jim. Before she was back with his dad and comfortable in her own skin. For a moment Riley had an uneasy flashback to the woman his mom had once been. In a designer dress and pearls, the scent of Chanel entered the room with her. All four men stood as she came in and she nodded to all of them before approaching Bill first.

"Bill, how wonderful to see you, how are Margaret and the children?"

"They are doing well." He leaned down for a peck on the cheek from the diminutive woman. He was all *aww shucks, ma'am* as he explained his eldest grandson had decided to come work with him and that he was now a great-grandaddy to a newborn that only arrived a few days ago.

She used the same treatment on Oscar but made no one feel like they were standing in line. Finally she pulled Ernst into a tight hug.

"I was so sorry to hear about Vera," she said softly.

Riley was attempting to not listen even as he, like the rest of the room, were wondering what Ernst's response was going to be. Vera, his wife of over forty years, had Alzheimer's, which was just another pressure the older man was dealing with.

She finally sat in one of the conference chairs and shrugged off her jacket. Steely eyed she looked right at Riley.

"So where are we at?"

Gone was the genteel oilman's wife and instead here was the woman Riley knew was under the mask. As she listened to what he said, and to what the others added, she was nodding and asking questions the likes of which Riley would have asked himself. Too many people underestimated the wife of an oilman.

Finally with all the information laid out in the arena, Sandra turned to him.

"So, how do we fix this, Riley?"

Ernst looked more comfortable with Sandra here and there was even a faint smile on his face. Sandra had that way about her. Not only that, but perhaps it was easier to deal with someone from the old guard as opposed to placing all his trust in a newcomer when there was any hint of doubt. Riley did wonder when he would be considered one of the old guard. When Hayley was coming up to thirty with children of her own perhaps?

"My concern is that we are already exposed to so much that if this went wrong..." Ernst shrugged.

Sandra sipped on her coffee and looked thoughtful. No one said anything for a second.

"Not one of us here can tell you what to do," she began. "What was it that drew you to joining this syndicate in the first place? Was it the chance to invest in something different? To work with Oscar, Bill, and Josiah?"

"All of those and none of them," Ernst answered honestly. "I'd heard good things about your son long before I met him." He turned so he faced Riley. "I remember talking to your father." He stopped and cast a look at Jim that screamed embarrassment. "Sorry, with Gerald, he said you had the instincts of an oilman. I think he saw it..." Ernst stopped talking.

"Go on," Sandra encouraged.

"As a curse. None of us ever understood why, not until everything happened." Again he cast a look at Jim and then at Sandra. "I trust Riley and CH Consulting, so for what it's worth," he paused as if to consider. Riley tensed as he waited. "Christex won't be pulling out of the syndicate."

Tension unknotted in Riley's chest. With that cleared there was only one thing to worry about—the government board assessing the bids. They talked for a long time and the coffee kept coming.

"We would need to approach the board and file a change in financing," Riley said. Tapping his pen against the papers, he considered what to say next. "We'll need new contracts drawn up—"

"Already on it," Jim said quickly. He didn't hang around.

"Then I guess we have nothing else to say, we just need to start doing," Riley said. He looked at his watch. The darkness outside the windows of the room indicated nighttime but he hadn't realized it was that late. "We need to formally dissolve the relationship with Josiah."

"And you probably need something to eat."

Riley looked up and blinked at the apparition in the doorway. Jack with a large box of Chinese food containers. He wasn't sure what he was more pleased to see, Jack in his worn jeans and pale blue shirt with a smile across his face or the food that scented the room.

Nah. There was no choice to be made. Quickly he pulled Jack into a hug and released him immediately. He wanted a kiss but he was in a room of businessmen. Jack smirked and then placed the containers on to the conference table. When everyone had a carton and they were eating, Riley glanced around at these men in their thousand dollar suits with their Rolexes and the air of authority that pervaded. Memories of Gerald and Jeff or not, Riley felt at home here. The shit would hit the fan when Josiah realized they had all sided with Riley—he was sure of it. But everything would be okay.

Especially with his mom and dad and Jack in his corner.

CHAPTER 16

"Robbie?" Eli had almost tiptoed up to Robbie in the hope he wouldn't see him coming and thus would not be able to avoid him. Three days now and Eli's cowboy was evidently nursing a grudge as big as Texas. Robbie didn't turn from what he was doing, but he did pause mid-movement with a huge steaming pile of horseshit on his shovel. For a second Eli winced. He could imagine him throwing the whole lot at him and Eli would deserve it. Robbie continued on to scoop the shit into a wheelbarrow but didn't acknowledge Eli.

"Robbie? Can we talk?" Eli said. He was trying for patience but if Robbie didn't say something soon then Eli would throw himself in the shit just so Robbie had to take notice of him.

"What about?"

Okay so that was a start. Right? At least Robbie was recognizing his presence. Now if only he could get Robbie to halt shoveling then that would help Eli stop focusing so much on the pull and stretch of worn jeans over Robbie's gorgeous ass and the play of muscles in his naked torso. Him not wearing a shirt should be outlawed here. What if someone else saw Robbie like this? All bare and slick with sweat?

"I got some of the cowboys from the rodeo to agree to a shoot here," Eli said firmly.

"I heard." *Still shoveling.*

"Will you stop that for a minute?" Eli's voice was maybe a bit more strident than he was aiming for but at least Robbie ceased moving. Instead he placed the shovel carefully on the floor and turned to face Eli. Running the back of his hand over his forehead was poetry in motion—the muscles and the skin, and the tattoo that marked his arm, and the chest definition. Eli swore he squeaked but Robbie didn't comment.

"Yes, sir," Robbie said instead.

What the hell? Sir?

"Robbie, don't—"

"Don't what?" Robbie's voice was deceptively calm but the glitter of anger flickered in his eyes.

"Look, I'm sorry."

"About cowboys coming here for a photo shoot?"

Was Robbie being deliberately dense? "About the other night."

"We're fine," he said. His voice was flat.

Eli took a step closer. No more than three feet separated them and Eli was close enough to see how damp Robbie's hair was. The air was humid today and a storm threatened. Eli loved the crash of thunder and the spears of lightening and at least if it broke the thick heated air then the ranch would be clean and cool tomorrow for the shoot.

"No, we're not fine," Eli offered. "You're right to be angry. I didn't think. That's half my problem, I never do. I shouldn't have even said you should go in that house and meet Michael, let alone have him pawing you."

"Glad to hear that," Robbie drawled.

Eli's dick was hardwired to that curious mix of drawling cowboy and Australia. He willed the damn thing to settle down but fuck if he wasn't hard the minute he looked at this man. He took another step forward. Maybe a foot in distance now, and Robbie didn't step back. Instead he reached out and placed a hand flat on top of Eli's, which was against his chest. Just like Riley had a few days before.

"Are you okay?" he said. Concern laced his voice.

Eli shook off his hand. "What is it with people asking me that?" Consciously he removed his hand from his chest.

"Because you do that thing." Robbie waved at the hand. "You push against your heart." His blue eyes held concern and for a second Eli considered playing on the unease. Was that the way to get through to Robbie? Maybe he should faint again like a freaking girl? Get big, strong Robbie to help him to bed?

"I'm fine," Eli said.

"You looked very pale for a second."

"I said I was fine. I was just contemplating fainting."

Alarm flashed on Robbie's face and this time his hand reached out but not in a gentle touch. Instead there was a strong grip to stop Eli from falling.

"We'll get you indoors," Robbie said.

"No." Eli pulled away from the hold and stumbled a few steps back. Reaching into the pocket of his loose jeans, he pulled out condoms and a travel pack of lube. "Don't baby me and treat me like I'm gonna break. Tell me you're over the shit I pulled and take me upstairs. Fuck me into tomorrow and tell me you want me."

Eli stopped. He had run out of dramatic statements. How else could he get Robbie to take him and get inside him and around him and forgive him for being a complete idiot?

Robbie stared. He really stared. First at the condoms then at the horses then back at Eli. He took a step toward Eli and all Eli could do was move back until he felt the wall behind him. There was something in Robbie that was alternately hot and terrifying. When Robbie was finally there, bracketing his hands around Eli's head and with his mouth next to Eli's ear he was whispering.

"Here? Should I take you here? Just turn you and push you up against the wall?"

"I don't know…" For all his bravery of just coming out and saying what he wanted, having Robbie this close was unnerving. He wanted everything and he wanted it now, but he'd thought they would go upstairs.

"Jack and Riley aren't in the house," Robbie stated simply.

Eli nodded. Neither man had made it home the night before, something to do with Riley's oil business. They were probably asleep at their desks at Riley's office.

"There's no chance of them walking in?" Eli asked.

"Here?" Robbie said. He shook his head. "No. We're taking this upstairs but before that, I have a question for you."

Eli writhed in Robbie's hold. "What?"

"Do you want to fuck me, or do you want a cowboy fucking you?"

Eli didn't even register the words as their tongues twisted in a thrust and pull of taste.

Inside me, he thought, *I want you inside me.* Robbie pressed closer and Eli couldn't stop the whimper that left him as he stopped kissing and murmured words into Eli's skin.

"I could fuck you till you beg to come," Robbie said. "I can do soft and slow where I use my hand to open you up, not just one finger, or two, but more, pushing and sliding slippery inside you? You want to kiss when we do it? Or just scream?"

"Robbie... fuck." Eli was so freaking hard and he wanted it all.

"I need to know before we do this, Eli. Do you want cowboy? Or do you want a gentleman? I can be either."

Eli processed the words. What was Robbie asking? Eli wanted hard and fast and then slow and steady, he wanted Robbie's work-roughened hands on him and he wanted to feel the smooth skin of Robbie's back under his touch. He wanted it all.

"Both," he said so gently that he repeated it in case Robbie hadn't heard. "I want the man who is both. I want you."

Robbie moved away and placed a hand on Eli's shoulder. Clearly he had passed some sort of weird Robbie test if the other man's soft smile was anything to go by.

"Hold that thought," he said. "Don't move."

Eli couldn't have moved if the barn were on fire.

* * * * *

Robbie finished the chores to get the horses sorted in ten minutes where it would have normally taken thirty. He would usually spend time talking to the horses, petting them and settling them but Eli had broken through every single barrier Robbie had with that simple statement. Eli had admitted he didn't want just any rough and ready cowboy taking him hard and fast, and he didn't want smooth and urbane and slick taking things slow. He wanted both. Eli said he wanted each part of him and, God help him, Robbie believed him.

Once finished, he went back to where Eli stood quiet and still. Robbie didn't want to talk and break anything they had sorted. He offered his hand, Eli took it, and Robbie guided the man up the outside stairs and into his small room. He couldn't remember what he had done to the bed this morning but at least it was kind of tidy. Eli didn't appear to care. As soon as the door was shut he was kissing Robbie. How they remained standing Robbie wasn't sure. Eli kissed like his life depended on it and didn't seem to want to stop for air. Robbie shoved at him slightly and Eli leaned back in.

"Slow down, we need to breathe," Robbie said. He aimed for teasing and was rewarded by Eli raising his eyebrows.

Eli muttered something under his breath that sounded like he didn't want to take his time but Robbie chuckled. "Let's take this horizontal," he said.

Eli got with that plan pretty quickly, shucking boots and jeans and a button-down until he stood in some pretty damn sexy shorts. Robbie followed suit but just a little slower. He was hot and sweaty from a day's work and really needed a shower. He wondered how that would go down with Eli and then inhaled sharply when Eli literally jumped him and overbalanced them both onto the bed.

"I was thinking about a shower—" Robbie started.

Eli wasn't having any of it. Experimentally he licked a stripe from Robbie's throat to a nipple, and suddenly a shower was right down the list of options if it meant he could get Eli biting and then laving his nipple like he was now.

"You taste like outside," Eli said. His voice was little more than a whisper. For a moment he sat upright, straddling Robbie's legs and just tracing Robbie's every muscle with his gaze.

"Something you like?" Robbie said. He had to break the intensity of Eli's concentration a little, and God, he wanted Eli's hands and mouth back on him.

Eli leaned forward and mutely requested more kisses by touch alone. "The minute I saw you I wanted you." He broke off from talking and trailed kisses to the other nipple.

Robbie pressed up into the touch and then sank his hands into Eli's hair. He wanted more of this. It had been too long. Tugging, he managed to get Eli up to lip level and stole more kisses. The lazy slide of tongues turned to more and when Eli moved his hand and pulled at Robbie's shorts, he was lost in sensation. The first touch of Eli's hand had Robbie moaning Eli's name. The lithe younger man was over him and tasting him, and sensation swirled inside Robbie. They were still kissing. Robbie had never had sex like this before. With Paul there were stolen moments when both were too exhausted to do anything more than get off, except for one memorable time in Brisbane when they had the whole weekend. That was when Robbie found out how much he liked slow and steady. The eroticism of preparation with the slide of fingers and the burn and the slick, slippery lube that trickled onto his balls was enough jerk-off material to last him a lifetime.

Robbie had never asked if Eli topped. Maybe he never did?

"Eli," Robbie said.

Eli looked up from where his mouth was leaving ovals of red skin where blood bloomed to the surface.

"When we're done, will you fuck me?"

Eli's eyes widened, but not because of the implications of the question it seemed. He lowered his gaze and for a moment, he was still.

Robbie hated the stillness and the sudden anxious look in Eli's eyes. "You don't have to—"

"I want to," Eli interrupted. "Thing is..." His voice trailed off and he laid his head on Robbie's chest, "I get tired."

"I'm sorry." The last thing Robbie wanted to do was to remind Eli of his illness or the lack of energy he said he sometimes felt. "I didn't mean—"

"No," Eli said with simple finality. He raised his head and locked gazes. "Give me an hour or so to recover then believe me, I would like nothing better than to get inside you." His voice was curiously husky. "First though. You in me. Now."

Robbie felt tension slip and it was replaced by the same arousal he had been feeling on and off ever since he met Eli. Just the man's voice was enough to send shivers down Robbie's spine and when they kissed it was as if they had never stopped to talk. With a practiced twist Robbie had

Eli on his back and there it was, his body laid out for Robbie to mark and use and love.

Dusk was darkening the room a little, blurring the edges, making every single touch and sigh more intimate and immediate. Robbie reached for his own lube—he wanted to do this right—Eli simply spread himself and tilted his hips in invitation.

Robbie sat up with his knees between Eli's legs, took the head of Eli's cock into his mouth, and the taste and weight of this man was perfect. Closing the gap between mouth and root with his lubed hand, he set up a rhythm that he knew could get Eli off if they wanted to. He stopped when moaning and pleading turned to little more than shallow breathing and tension made Eli's thighs rock solid. Taking his lubed hand to Eli's ass, he pressed there and pushed inside. Just one finger. Enough to spread lube inside and crook to touch the nerve-filled sensitive channel. Eli moaned and Robbie felt Eli's fingers grazing Robbie's lips and pressing inside his mouth.

Robbie groaned at the feeling—of Eli touching himself while Robbie was tasting—and he couldn't bring himself to tell Eli not to touch his own dick. The way this was going Eli was going to come hard and fast without Robbie even getting a look in. That was fine. Impossibly, it was evident he was really only focused on Eli, which was a new sensation. A second finger joined the first with his thumb pressing the taint between ass and balls. The pressure there was evidently an overload as Eli turned from merely breathing to guttural begging. The lube was slippery slick and he pushed a third finger deeper inside Eli. God, Robbie wanted inside and he wanted it now.

Lifting his wet lips from the end of Eli's cock, he left with a broad swipe of his tongue across Eli's hand and to his balls—Eli's ass lifted off the bed, giving Robbie the best view he had ever seen. Eli was begging and twisting his head as Robbie pressed the P-spot and sent Eli higher. Eli's hand was closed around his own dick but he wasn't moving his hand, simply pressing it flat against his hip bone. Robbie hurriedly rolled a condom on himself, hissing when the touch of it against his sensitive skin nearly made him come there and then.

He moved until his knees supported Eli's upper thighs, and with no words he pushed the broad head of his dick against Eli's slippery wet hole. The pressure was intense and Robbie saw Eli shut his eyes.

"Sorry if I hurt you." He groaned as he pushed through the ring of tight muscle and beyond.

"Not… hurting…" Eli muttered. His face screwed up with concentration and Robbie waited until the expression eased. When it had he pressed forward and finally, when Eli's body allowed him to, he was balls deep in the sexiest man he had ever seen. Eli groaned and opened his eyes wide.

"You need to move," he said.

Robbie looked into his beautiful green eyes and then to his hands gripping the white sheets tightly.

"Are you okay?" he asked.

"Get on with it, you fucker," Eli griped.

Robbie chuckled and pulled out a little before pushing back in. Gently he continued to do this until he saw Eli's breathing settled into a rhythm he could match. This wasn't going to take long. Robbie leaned over as best he could to kiss. He loved kissing while fucking. It meant he was close enough to taste Eli and hear the delicious sounds he was making.

Orgasm twisted low in him. The tingle of being so near and edging, then pulling nearly out and waiting was as near damn perfect as anything.

"I need…" Eli said around the kisses.

"What? What do you need, Eli?"

"Harder." Eli's hand was running the length of his dick and pre-cum lightened the end as he drew his fingers up and over.

Robbie was happy to comply and he shifted slightly so he had a steady base. Moving this way meant he could go deeper, harder, push more. The pace was punishing and the sweat he had worked up outside with the horses was nothing on the sheen of moisture on his and Eli's skin. A minute, nothing more, and Eli arched with a muffled shout and was coming across his belly with Robbie following soon after from the delicious tensing of Eli's muscles around him.

For a second they stayed still, blue gaze meeting green, and the high of orgasm thick in the air. As he softened, Robbie gripped the end of the condom and dropped it to the floor by the bed. He could deal with it in a minute when he actually had some energy.

Still panting heavily, he slumped to one side and moved his hands above his head.

"Fuck, Eli," was all he could manage.

"That was…" Eli was boneless, sprawled over his half of the bed with a blissed-out expression on his face.

"Best. Sex. Ever," Robbie replied. He was not lying. He couldn't remember feeling as wiped out and high when he'd had sex. Eli begging and pleading and then having him writhing under him had literally blown his mind.

"Not sex… I love you," Eli murmured.

Robbie couldn't help tensing at the words. *Love is dangerous. It makes you plant roots where maybe you don't want any.*

"Don't say things like that," Robbie half whispered.

"You can't stop me from saying I love you." Eli sounded incredulous. "Doesn't matter what you think back, I just want you to know that I want more of this. I don't just want sex."

"I'm leaving at the end of the season." Robbie kept his thoughts to himself about whether or not he could bring himself to leave the Double D, Eli or no Eli. "No point in making plans and promises past Christmas."

"Guess not," Eli said.

His tone was very even and Robbie was thankful Eli wasn't going all possessive on him. The sex was good. Hell, the sex was awesome. And who could blame him if he wanted to pull Eli in for a cuddle just about now. Post-sex cuddling wasn't on his list of things to avoid in life. He had to avoid falling in love again. That was number one.

Eli didn't say anything else. He rolled on to his side and rested his head on Robbie's chest, settling in close and falling asleep really quickly. When he was convinced that Eli was deeply under, he eased himself out of bed and pulled on his jeans and boots. He just needed to check the horses before he could really settle to sleep. He opened the door and the cool evening air slapped at his room-hot body and he smiled. There was nothing better than the touch of breeze that stirred the night.

"Everything okay?"

Robbie looked down at the fencing close to the barn. Jack leaned against the wood and looked up at him. He guessed the shit was going to hit the fan in the end but still he was hoping maybe he and Eli could go at least a few nights without having to sneak around and be watched.

"Yeah," he answered. Taking the steps two at a time he stopped at the bottom. His heart wanted to go straight to the horses; his head told him Jack's presence near his place was maybe an indication he wanted to talk.

"Is Eli asleep?"

Robbie leaned against the same fence with his booted foot up on the lower level. He could play this one of two ways: *Yes, Eli is asleep,* or *no, I don't know.*

"Yeah." No sense in beating around the bush.

"You come down to check the horses?"

"I always do, one last time before I go to bed."

"I know. I see you most nights. You're good with them. Good for the ranch."

"Thank you." Never let it be said Robbie Curtis didn't know a compliment when it was given by the guy who paid his wages.

"I was hoping to catch you tonight." Jack turned so his back was to the fence and he rested his elbows back on the wood. Tipping his head back to look up at the sky he continued. "You said you were thinking of moving on after Christmas and I was wondering if maybe you had given any thought to staying on."

"I hadn't."

"I'd like you to. I have a proposition for you. I know you have the bonuses for the training but I would like to suggest that maybe we had something more concrete in place. More of a partnership in the new horses we train up."

Robbie was lost for words. He'd seen this done before; where trainers partnered and shared rewards. What Jack was proposing was a lot more than just simple bonuses but an actual chance to make some serious money doing what he loved.

"I don't have the money to stake my share."

Jack shrugged. "I would cover your share and you could pay it back out of proceeds."

Jack made it sound so simple. If only his damned head would get itself out of this cycle of moving on then maybe this would be the perfect choice. Images of Eli asleep in his bed, sprawled this way and that in tangled sheets, passed through Robbie's thoughts. If he stayed at the Double D longer, if he actually put down a root or two, then the other thing he would need to consider is where Eli fit into all of this. Saying that he loved Robbie was like a burr under a saddle; it itched and scratched and wouldn't go away.

"Think on it," Jack said simply.

Robbie nodded. "I will."

Jack pushed himself away from the fence and began to walk back to the main house.

"Jack?" Robbie called and Jack stopped to turn and face him. "Thank you for your faith in me." He felt heat in his face; he wasn't used to making such sweeping grand statements of thanks.

"Let me know when you make a decision."

And with that Jack left Robbie propping up the fence and with a head full of ifs, buts, and maybes.

The horses done, he went back to Eli, who rolled over and clung to him as soon as he climbed into bed. The last time he had slept with someone, or invested any time in someone, had been with Paul. Losing Paul was damn near close enough to having his heart ripped from his chest.

He slid his hand down Eli's side, resting finally on the obvious scar where Robbie stroked a pattern of indecision. Paul had a weakness inside him, his brain had a fault, and now Robbie met Eli who had cancer, which also hides deep in the body. Could Robbie stand to let himself fall again? Was it possible to love another man and not fear every day that fate was going to rip them apart?

Staying at the Double D, partnering with Jack, drawing a line and making his stand in the dirt? That all involved Eli at some point in the equation.

Eli Martin with his dark hair that was soft against Robbie's skin and his forest green eyes that sparked with life and hope.

When did I lose that same life? That same hope?

Eli moved again in sleep, his hand curling across Robbie's chest and then reflexively relaxing, and Robbie tightened his grip on the man.

Lying in his arms was the most danger his heart had ever faced.

CHAPTER 17

"Everything okay?" Riley said from under the sheet. All that Jack could see of his husband was the tufts of blond hair and the distinctive shape of six foot four inches of man on the bed. Yesterday and into today had been tough all round so there was no wonder Riley was hiding away from light and turning into a mushroom. What Josiah had done was reminiscent of the type of crap Gerald had pulled. The same kind of thing Riley's brother Jeff had done, casting doubt, making up shit that looked official. There was a meeting at eleven with attorneys and legal aides and everyone else from the directory of legal support. Thankfully it was here, but still, Riley was exhausted.

"Everything's fine. I waited for Robbie. Go to sleep, we can talk in the morning."

"What did he say?" Riley's face appeared from under the sheet and he blinked at the soft light from the bedside lamp. "Did he agree to stay at the Double D for the long term?"

"Not exactly. But he didn't say no, just that he would think on it."

"He's never stayed in one place for longer than a year, not since his boyfriend died. I'm not sure he thinks he *can* stay here."

"We have another few months. Maybe we can convince him."

"We can try."

"Eli was up in Robbie's room."

"Was he?"

Jack knew it wasn't that Riley disbelieved what he said. They had both wondered how Eli would manage to wear Robbie down enough to get in his bed.

"Robbie had a way about him tonight. He was relaxed and happy. I think Eli would be good for him."

Riley's cell chirped and he looked over at their clock. Jack passed it to him—Riley had to answer. CH and the new syndicate were less than forty-eight hours from a decision on the rights and they still had the thorny issue of making sure the new bid was locked down legally so that it would just be the four of them, no longer including Josiah after he showed his colors on the rival bid. Riley was lucky if he was going to get enough sleep before tomorrow's meeting let alone over the next two days. He looked a little gray and way beyond exhausted.

"Eden?"

Jack unashamedly listened in. Eden calling was a very different thing to one of the syndicate calling, or a representative, or a lawyer. Jack generally drifted away on his own thoughts when Riley went into oilman mode.

"Okay. Calm down. Have you called Mom? Dad... Jim?"

"What's wrong?" Jack interrupted.

Riley held up a hand and Jack bit his tongue. Riley nodded and then ended the call with an, 'I'll be right there'.

"Where? Where are we going to be?" If Riley said he was going somewhere and looked this damned serious then Jack was going too.

"It's Sean," Riley explained. He too was dressing in record time and he grabbed his phone, wallet, watch, and keys from the bedside table. "He was caught in some kind of trouble. I don't know any more. Eden wasn't making sense. We're meeting them at Mercy."

The hospital? What the hell has happened?

"Some kind of fight. I don't know, Eden couldn't get the words out."

* * * * *

As soon as Riley went through security, Eden was there. She nearly threw herself at him and he held her as close as he could.

"What happened?" Jack asked.

"We'd gone out for dinner—he's going away tomorrow—was—we were waiting for a table and these photographers came over and Sean just lost his temper. I've never seen him so angry. There was a fight and he smashed a camera. They had to pull him off and he was shouting all these things about men dying and..." Her steam ran out and Riley helped her through a door marked families and encouraged her to the first chair.

A quick scan revealed the room was empty and Jack stood against the door, guarding it with arms crossed over his broad chest.

Riley turned his sister's face with a gentle touch, two butterfly bandages closing a cut on her face.

"What happened to you?"

"It was Sean. He—"

She didn't even finish. Riley was on his feet and at the door in seconds with murder in his heart. Jack blocked his way.

"Let her finish," Jack said.

Riley thought about arguing for a second but then Eden was talking and as Riley listened the horror inside him rose.

"He didn't mean to. He wouldn't hurt me, Riley. He loves me. There was broken glass, a mirror I think, and someone came at me. Sean pushed me to one side and took the full force of the remains of the mirror." She touched her face. "This..." Her voice broke. "This was nothing. Riley... he's... Sean's face, his eye."

Riley crossed to his sister.

"Where is he now?"

"Surgery. They..." Eden's face crumpled and she buried her face in her hands.

Riley couldn't hear anything else. He held his little sister tightly as she sobbed against his chest. Her story didn't make a lot of sense. Sean was the most gentle of guys and for all of Riley's big brother protectiveness about this whole Afghanistan thing he was a good guy. Whether or not he was the right guy for Eden? Hell, Riley was the first to admit he had a skewed perspective. It's what big brothers did.

A fight? Glass, a mirror, and Sean losing his temper? And now in surgery for damage to what? His eye? His face.

"Shall I go and see what I can find out?" Jack said softly.

Riley doubted that Eden heard Jack and he simply nodded. Maybe if they had the entire story then some of this would make more sense.

Five minutes after Jack was gone Jim and Sandra arrived. Evidently Eden had called them as well, and finally with a few exchanged words about what the hell was going on they fell silent. Sandra sat next to her daughter stroking her back and whispering words of reassurance, Jim was pacing.

"Jack went to find out what is happening," Riley explained.

"There's police outside. He's talking to them," Jim said. "They'll want to speak to Eden but I explained she wasn't well. I'm not sure how long they will wait."

Riley nodded and gently eased Eden away from him. She looked white, the cut on her forehead standing out in stark relief against her pale skin. Her eyes looked impossibly green against the red from crying and she was looking at Riley like he may have all the answers.

"You up to talking to the cops?" Riley asked gently.

"It's my fault, Riley. If I hadn't kept secrets... if Jeff... the Universe is paying me back."

Riley stopped her then with a gentle shake. Christ, if anyone heard her saying this stuff and put two and two together to make five then secrets buried with Gerald Hayes and the real identity of who killed Jeff would be too close to the surface to hide. Fear knifed through Riley and the hushed silence in the room was absolute. What if his sister mentioned the name Lisa and the fact it had been her who had killed Jeff?

"Stop that now," he said firmly. "You don't say stuff like that. Ever. You hear me?"

"Riley?" She was crying again, huge, wrenching sobs that forced their way from her heart. "I need to know what's happening to Sean."

"Jack will find out," Sandra interrupted. "Let's get you taken care of, sweetheart." Sandra had her no-nonsense mom voice going on and she turned to Jim. "You take Riley outside and stall them. Eden and I will be out in a few minutes."

Riley stood and let his dad out of the room first. If anyone could school Eden in how to keep secrets it was their mom. If anyone found out it was Lisa who had pulled the trigger and killed her husband… it didn't bear thinking about. Riley had grown so blasé about it all—it was such a long time ago and there were so many reasons Lisa had snapped. When she heard what Jeff said, how he had raped Jack's sister, Beth, how he was hurting her and other, much younger, girls, she had been pushed over the edge. Riley didn't judge Lisa but had somehow compartmentalized everything that had happened like it was unimportant. If Eden said anything about their brother? How could he have just pushed his concerns to one side like that? There needed to be damage limitation on a daily basis and he needed to keep his eye on the ball.

They exited straight into chaos.

Jack was standing firm, guarding the door from the other side. His feet were firmly planted on the white floor and his legs spread a little. He was not going to be moved. Riley met his gaze and Jack nodded. Jack had this handled and for that Riley loved his husband even more. He could rely on Jack one hundred percent. Total and absolute support.

"We need to get in there to speak to Eden Hayes." The uniformed cop looked like he wanted to be in a million other places than this one. He was sweating, red-faced, and had the look of a man on the edge.

"She'll be out in a minute," Riley said.

"Sir—"

"She'll. Be. Out. In. A. Minute." Riley repeated each word clearly, and stood shoulder to shoulder with Jack. "What's the situation, Jack?" he asked.

"Sean's back in a room. Surgery was good. He's handcuffed to the bed on suspicion of assault. He's unconscious and likely to be so for the next twenty-four hours."

Riley heard every word and as each piece of news hit him he wondered what the fuck they had wandered into here. Jim intervened. Gently but firmly he guided the cop away, in full-on lawyer mode instantly. Citing one of many provisos and addendums and codes that went right over Riley's head, made the cop go from agitated to respectful in a second. When two more officers arrived, neither in uniform, Riley recognized one of them as the cop involved in Jeff's murder case. Stone or something. Great. Just fucking great.

"Riley Campbell-Hayes," he held out a hand which Riley shook, "Detective Tom Stafford." The other cop with him was in conversation with the uniform and Jim.

"Why is a Dallas PD homicide detective involved in this?" To Riley's knowledge no one had died.

Tom shrugged. "I was just passing. Heard there was a Hayes involved. You know I have a special interest in your family and wondered if I could help." He didn't elaborate any further.

"For a start you can un-cuff my sister's fiancé unless you are arresting unconscious people."

"Procedure, Mr Campbell-Hayes. Sean Harris was seen threatening a fellow patron at a restaurant—"

"Some reporters from a dirt magazine," Riley spat.

"With all due respect, everyone, regardless of their career choices, are as worthy of our protection as the next man."

Riley doubted that but he didn't say. No point in arguing any defense—that wasn't why he was here.

The door to the family room opened and a composed Eden exited, following closely by Sandra.

"Miss Hayes." Tom stepped forward. "I wonder if I might ask a few questions."

Riley watched his sister visibly draw herself tall and inhale and exhale deeply before she simply said.

"Of course."

CHAPTER 18

Robbie shut his cell with a look of determination on his face.

"What did he say?" Eli asked.

They had moved into the main house when Jack had asked them to sit with Hayley while they went at the hospital to find out what had happened.

"Not much. Just that we should just stay here with Hayley and would we mind babysitting for the next few hours. He says he's going to get Riley back home as soon as he can."

Eli checked his watch. "The rodeo guys will be here in an hour for the shoot."

"Can I help you?" Hayley wandered into the kitchen and clambered into her chair.

Eli's photographer eyes could see the beauty in Hayley. With Riley's hazel-green eyes and the elfin shape to her face he knew Riley would be daddy to one hell of a heartbreaker. She was taking the news about her Aunty Eden and Sean, the man she called uncle, very well. As far as she was concerned her daddies were handling it and in her world that was more than enough. Having seen the two men together Eli didn't dismiss this. They were formidable as a couple.

"Of course you can, sweetheart. I'll need someone to assist me and my friend Lauren with telling the guys where to stand. You want to do that?"

"Yes, please. Oh, and can I bring my own camera? Pappa said I could use his anytime I wanted."

"Go fetch it and we'll make sure it's all charged up."

A knock on the door heralded the entrance of Lauren, who had arrived with the van of equipment. She was a whirlwind of organization and when the stylist arrived it was all systems go.

"How are you going to keep it in your pants today?" Lauren whispered as they walked toward the six models clustered around one of the horses on the Double D.

Eli caught sight of Robbie in the middle of them all, animated as he discussed horses and whatever the hell else he was an expert in. Robbie's face was all smiles, and his body language was relaxed. Eli had never actually seen his cowboy as loose as this, apart from after the frankly awesome sex.

Love. In Eli's mind he was making love. Let Robbie have his little fantasy that this was just sex and that he was leaving the ranch, and indeed Texas, at the end of the year. Eli had another three months to persuade him to stay.

"Not interested," he answered.

"Six buff and au naturel cowboys and you don't think you are going to get a taste. Who are you kidding?" Lauren was incredulous.

Eli shrugged. Why would she think any different? All Lauren had seen in him in the three years they had been working together was short-term hookups.

"I have my own cowboy," he said. "Why would I want another one?"

They had reached the group by then and Eli switched into photographer mode. If only every man was as lucky as to tell six cowboys to strip to their underwear in the barn.

For the fact the guys weren't streetwise models Lauren kept out of the way and allowed them to undress and dress in peace but the stylist was itching to get her hands on all of them.

"I don't want them ruined," Eli had argued.

"Just some foundation to—"

"No."

"Haircuts?"

"I'm not photographing faces. This is torso, legs, and ass work."

In fact he did end up catching the entire cowboy each time. But they wore Stetsons—real ones that were colored with age—and faces were in shadow. He grouped them on a fence and shot upward against the crisp blue sky or took them singly one by one to stand with horses. Hayley mimicked his actions and made friends with the cowboys, the absolute center of attention. She loved it and it took her mind off of where her daddy and pappa were.

When they had finished for the day Eli was excited about the shots he had achieved, and he sent a few of the raw images off to Michael and his team. The feedback he had almost straight away was positive with some suggestions. Nothing that meant re-shooting the men, only improvements that could be made for color in the editing stage.

Finally only Lauren remained and she was loading the van up with the equipment that needed storing.

"So, he's the one then? The guy, Robbie, who was hanging around."

"He's the one," Eli said.

"He's hot." She smirked.

Eli laughed. Yes he was hot in his low-slung jeans with the sweat of work sheening his body and his muscles bunching and relaxing as he worked. But there was more to Robbie than that.

"Yeah. He's my forever man. The one I can see waking up next to until the day I die." He hesitated for a moment, "Whenever that is."

"You love him?"

"Yeah." His voice softened. "His heart is so big and I know if I could show him how good we can be that he'd see he was able to love me too."

"What if I do already?"

Eli spun on his feet. Robbie was maybe a foot or so behind him and Lauren was smirking.

"I'm gone," she said. With an air kiss she was away from the ranch in a cloud of dust.

Finally Eli and Robbie were alone standing in the yard in front of the ranch.

"What do you mean?"

"What if, and God knows how you did this, what if you already made me think I should be staying here past the year and giving us the chance to see where this goes?"

"You just said..." Eli couldn't form the words. He had heard right, hadn't he?

"I said what if I already did love you?"

"You did," Eli confirmed. Hope bloomed inside him.

"I was watching you when you were working with the guys today. They respected you. Couple of them called you hot and wondered if you were gay. I didn't like it."

Disappointment chased away the hope.

"So," Eli said. "Just jealousy then? You want something they wanted."

Robbie chuckled and took a step forward. "You look like a kid that was promised a pony and was given a wooden horse." He cupped Eli's face and pressed a gentle kiss to Eli's forehead.

Robbie continued. "It sure as hell opened my eyes. So I spent the day watching you. The way you smile and laugh, the way you encouraged Hayley, the jokes you shared with Lauren, and I saw underneath all the cocky confidence."

"Shit. You did?"

"You're my kind of guy, Elijah Martin."

Eli wrapped his hands around the back of Robbie's neck and pulled him in for a kiss.

"So is this saying that you are staying now? Or am I following you around the country?"

"I'm thinking I might. Wanna move into a one-room apartment over a barn?"

"And give up my expensive sterile loft with its hot and cold running maid service? Hell yes."

They kissed deeply and the emotion that had been building inside of Eli burst out in a slash of passion and want.

"Eli! Robbie! I got cola out for us!"

Hayley's not so little voice echoed over the yard and the two men reluctantly pulled apart. Hand in hand they walked to the ranch house and a smiling Hayley.

"I'm falling in love with you, Eli," Robbie whispered.

Eli squeezed his hand.

He was already there.

* * * * *

Riley stood at the end of Sean's bed. At least the cuffs had been removed and he was lying peacefully, oblivious to the shit storm that he had incited.

"Why didn't he just take you somewhere else? When he knew that they were following you?"

"They weren't. Following me, that is." Eden crossed to sit in the chair next to Sean's bed and folded one of his hands in hers. "I was just an added bonus, but they took their photos and then went to the bar. When Sean went to the restroom… Look, I don't know what happened, but one of them must have said or done something, because when I watched him walk back I saw him stop and turn to one of them. They could have said something about me, I don't know, but Sean was shouting and it was more about soldiers and dying. I told all this to the police."

"Go on." Riley wanted to hear it all and this was as good a time to hear it.

"He hasn't been the same since he came back from his last research trip to Afghanistan. He's due to fly out the day after tomorrow for his final visit, but the closer it came the tenser he was getting. His eyes…" She stopped and bowed her head.

Riley could hear tears in her voice and it broke his heart.

"What about his eyes, Eden?" he asked gently.

"They were sometimes so haunted. He wouldn't talk about what he had seen, just spoke of the friends he had made and the things that he thought would make me smile.

I know he didn't tell me everything but I didn't push. Some nights he would not be able to sleep and I would wake at three and he would be sitting with his laptop, getting his words on paper. Not the fluid tap of keys but an almost aggressive writing—I can't explain. He would shut the laptop and smile at me. But his eyes never smiled."

"I'm sorry, Eden."

Eden shuffled the chair a little closer and rested her face against Sean's chest, being careful to avoid the cannula and tube that was connected to a drip. The entire left side of his face from eye to chin was bandaged. Eden had said there was a lot of blood and she couldn't see the damage but Riley had heard the doctor talk to her. Words like blind, and loss of sight, and nerve damage were thrown about like they meant nothing.

"Do you need anything?" he asked.

Eden looked up at him. "No. Thank you."

Sean had protected Eden when she had come to see what was happening. A mirror had smashed and was half hanging on the wall. When one of the photographers had moved and she was pushed toward it, something had made Sean twist and shield her as the mirror fell and it had sliced into his face. The horror of it made Riley sick. Whatever started the fight, whoever was to blame, Sean had protected Eden to the end. For that Riley would forever be grateful. Now they just needed to know what the hell had caused it all.

CHAPTER 19

Riley shifted and lifted the covers when Jack came back to bed. It was the way things were between them. The rhythm of Jack's breathing and the reassurance of him being in bed were the only two things Riley depended on. They were what he needed so badly tonight and he couldn't sleep without them.

"Horses okay?" he asked as Jack slipped off his clothes and climbed into bed. In seconds they were in each other's arms, in the perfect position, with Jack resting his face on Riley's chest.

They lay in silence for a while and Riley's thoughts played havoc with his breathing. Sean was awake but groggy. It appeared that the photographers had made some comment about the war and Sean had seen just enough to want to make a stand.

Sean had lost a friend that day. A corporal that had been assigned as his guide had been killed by a roadside bomb. That was why the argument started. No one, it seemed, was pressing charges—not one photographer in the group of four came forward and admitted to what had been said, despite witnesses close by telling it exactly as it had been. Christ knows what would happen down the road though.

There was no way about it, Sean had lost his sight in one eye. The optic nerve was severed, the damage too severe. It didn't matter how much money Eden or Riley could throw at the situation, Sean was not going to heal. The scarring on his face could be dealt with, according to the plastic surgeon who had attended him today. Riley was there when Sean just closed his good eye and shook his head. Eden looked at Riley helplessly. Sean would need help to get his head around all of this but at least he wasn't pushing Eden away. Yet.

"Did Stafford talk to you after I left the hospital?" Jack asked.

The detective had been waiting at reception when Jack left and had cornered Riley.

"He didn't say much. Just explained that Sean was free to go when he was well."

Jack settled under the covers and pulled Riley in close.

"Are you still thinking about the bid?"

Riley would be lying if he said he wasn't thinking about the fact CH had won the bid, but in the grand scheme of things it was less important than what his sister was going through.

"I'm pleased... and surprised."

"Bet Josiah is spitting nails."

"Dad thinks they will file to say our new syndicate isn't stable."

"Do they have a case?"

Riley sighed. He wished he had an answer. After what happened with Eden's almost slip-up about the memories of Jeff and Gerald, Riley realized he wasn't anxious about Josiah or anything that would come of this. He had bigger things that should be occupying his thoughts. Eden had been close to losing her control in hospital, and saying what she said could have been heard. Secrets nearly spilled and he couldn't sleep even after Jack was breathing rhythmically. Deliberately he turned his thoughts from the black pit of his family history to his friend Eli and the growing relationship between him and Robbie.

When they got home after dinner Eli was with Robbie, Hayley, and the horses. Eli said the shoot had gone well and that Hayley had been his assistant. Eli had been Hayley's babysitter and judging by the elaborate hair twist up on her head, he was clearly better than Riley with women's hair. Either that or the stylist for the models had been involved. Eli was settled here. The natural progression went from thinking about Eli and how Robbie was a good man and in particular one of the best things to happen to Eli ever. Riley imagined converting some of the older buildings some distance from the main house into a more permanent place for Robbie if he stayed. Family was important.

"Jack? You asleep?"

"Mnnh." Jack was very clearly in sleep zone.

"Do you think Hayley would like a sister or brother?"

Silence. Complete and absolute silence. Riley could have kicked himself. Jack would probably think this was a stupid idea. Hell, he'd taken Hayley on like his own but that didn't mean he wanted a whole ranch of rug rats. Who was he kidding anyway? They were two gay men with careers. What did they know about having another child? Maybe a baby? Who knew what to do with a baby?

"A baby. you mean?" Jack said finally.

"I don't know. Not necessarily. Never mind. We can talk later." Riley wanted the conversation finished. Last thing he needed was to be pressuring Jack into things they didn't need.

"I want to talk now," Jack said.

He didn't sound pissed. Thoughtful and considering maybe, but not angry.

"Okay?" Riley said carefully. He wondered what Jack was going to say.

"I've been thinking on this a lot."

"You have?" *So have I.*

"How would you feel if we tried for surrogacy first? With me as the donor?" Jack sounded hesitant.

Riley shrugged free of Jack and leaned over to turn on the light until the low wattage filled the room. Jack was blinking in the light and appeared as uncertain as his voice had indicated. Riley couldn't get his words out fast enough.

"A boy with your blue eyes and your ornery stubbornness or a girl who could become the best barrel racer ever seen? Do you mean this for real?" Suddenly the world seemed brighter, like Riley could take on everything and come out winning.

Jack half smiled. "I do."

Riley whooped his approval and clambered to straddle Jack, pushing him flat on the bed.

"Fuck, Jack, I love you."

Jack grinned up at him. "Het-boy? You know what?"

"What?"

"I love you too."

The End

CONNECT WITH RJ

RJ Scott lives just outside London. She has been writing since age six, when she was made to stay in at lunchtime for an infraction involving cookies and was told to write a story. Two sides of A4 about a trapped princess later, a lover of writing was born. She loves reading anything from thrillers to sci-fi to horror; however, her first real love will always be the world of romance. Her goal is to write stories with a heart of romance, a troubled road to reach happiness, and more than a hint of happily ever after.

Email: rj@rjscott.co.uk
Webpage: www.rjscott.co.uk
Facebook: author.rjscott
Twitter: rjscott_author